AHMED EL MARAKBY

PRINCIPLES & DIGNITY

FOR SALE

The Story of the unknown novelist

Based on a true story of the writer's life.

A personal view of London, the city and life in the UK

Alex D:

When I first met Oscar a few years ago, I could see he was an interesting character, but it took me months of talking to him to realize how interesting. The first stories he told me only scratched the surface of something much deeper. When he told me of his past, I could scarcely believe it. Though much of his life has been outside the realm of usual human experience, there is something that rings true to me. I hope you find his tale as enlightening as I have and still do.

Micol C:

A powerful story that engages, amuses, moves and gives pause for thought. A book of strong feelings, vivid metaphors and brilliant ideas that will drive readers to run away from the bars of their cage, because everything is possible if you try hard, and that's Oscar's lesson and it is definitely worth reading.

Contents

Introduction

In early August 2013, Alex D was the 18-year-old, British boy who started working with us in (H), the most luxurious retailer in the world, in Knightsbridge, one of the largest and most luxurious places in the world, delivering the smile and (H) experience to the rich and famous people from all over the place, including, celebrities, footballers, actresses and even politicians.

I was a senior brand ambassador at that time and Alex was one of the new school-leavers that had joined us in early 2013. We were working as a team in one of the most expensive and luxurious brands in the world.

Alex and I, in our free time, used to share our thoughts, personal opinions and discuss our vision of life and the future.

Alex was a very talented young man, with a bright mind, excellent performance and a sophisticated character. I was so impressed to find all these qualities in someone of such a young age, like Alex and quickly Alex became the top person on my list of people that I chat openly with.

At that time I was shining in my career and I was awarded, twice in a row, the personality of the year achievement for 2012 and 2013. I was such a successful salesman, with a natural attitude, in the most sensitive and valuable department in (H). Also my feedback and reputation were speaking for me, as I was quite a poplar and beloved person.

Once Alex asked me, "What is your secret? What's behind your unique character and success?" He was surprised when I explained to him how simple I am and how complicated my life was.

I told him about my journey when I was fighting for my life to win back, at an auction, all my personal valuables that I'd lost when I was a gambler. I'd been gambling my own principles and dignity after they had been sold in the auction of life.

"I like the way you talk and the way you analyse things! Have you ever thought about writing?" Alex said.

I smiled with a sad look and suddenly I felt like someone had touched an old wound. I felt like I was being captured and dragged on a roller coaster, and like a hurricane, being taken back to my past.

I looked at Alex and in a sad, low tone I said to him, "In fact, I used to write a lot and writing for me was a way of escaping my blues. I also studied novel, drama, poetry and philosophy for five years."

Alex was surprised and started to wonder deeply, what would make me stop writing and why hadn't I start writing again!

In fact it was not only Alex who'd asked me to write my story down on paper. Alex was one of thousands of people who were persistently asking me to write my mysterious story down. But I always refused the idea, as I always believed that my story couldn't be shared for a few reasons: first, I did not want people to feel or show any kind of sympathy. Secondly, I thought who would care to read a dramatic story nowadays in such a takeaway world?

I also was not sure that I would be able convert my feelings into words, using my poor English and even if I could, I was still having my doubts about who would care and spend the time to read a book by someone unknown like me. I was not an actor, or a celebrity, or even famous, but what people did not know was that in my own story I actually was!

I could not figure out why Alex insisted on knowing my story. Perhaps he was just curious, or he might be bored and was looking for some entertainment to pass the time. But after a long conversation with Alex, especially when I told him that the brand manger and the personality of the year who was standing in front of him was once actually homeless, Alex was interested to know more and more.

I also realized that Alex and I had too many things in

common. And as I always believe that everyone we meet in our life has a secret story, a hidden wound or family issues, I knew Alex had his.

Additionally I was surprised when he revealed to me that he was a writer too and he was halfway through his own book.

Alex assured me that I was making a great mistake for not sharing my story.

He said to me, "There are some people out there who deserve to learn from our experiences and what we have been through. There are some people, who are willing to take life journeys, but they have a fear of controlling them and perhaps they may need a story to read, such as yours, as motivation. People fear changes or moving on. There are some people out there who need to know that whatever mistakes they make they cannot always blame circumstances. Circumstances cannot be used as excuses. Circumstances cannot judge or control your future, or your personal situations. In fact it does, with weak people who have not got enough determination.

"But we have the option to choose what we want to be. No one else is responsible for our choices. And dreams still can be reached and come true, and miracles still can happen, whatever the time or the generation. All we need to do is to give it a try."

Alex said, sharing my story could change someone's life, or benefit someone who was lost or confused in life. And not sharing it was kind of selfish of me.

I said to Alex, I did not want people to feel sympathy, or to feel sorry for me!

He said, "I think it is the other way around and I am sure it is you who feels sympathy for people, as you already made it and look who you became. You were strong, you fought and you made it through." Alex ended his thoughtful words by saying, "At least there are some people around you who love you to death and they deserve to be a part of your life. It is their right to have access to your life's gallery."

I was so touched by Alex's words, especially when he offered to be my private editor for my book. He also convinced me that my buried library could be revealed and my stories could be cleaned and wiped up, and made ready to welcome new visitors.

But the worst part for me was the idea of holding my old rusty pen again and it was not an easy decision for me to make. Perhaps I did not know how to start, or where to begin.

Or maybe I was just scared of going back to the place where my memories were hidden and having to start to dig, plus I didn't want to remember the past that I was always trying to run or recover from.

And here my story began...

The Prince of Sadness

Prince of Sadness was the name which had been given to me by the people who surrounded me in the past and who were also witnesses to my story. They said that name suited me, especially when I couldn't escape and cut myself loose from my bleeding heart of the past; the past that followed me wherever I went. Even after I reached my final destination, it was always there to remind me and my remaining scars, about our permanent contract.

Our contract was never-ending. I thought it would be temporary at the beginning, but apparently it seemed to be for a lifetime. People say that wounds can heal with time, but for me, time was the only thing I wanted to end or to kill. I remembered when my tears invaded my eyes and took over a place that would be their new home; even when I tried to let them free! They resisted and built their own cage. Pain was my mate, it also kept me company instead of a normal partner – we suffered together in silence, living together in a freehold property made of blues located in my heart, let and managed by dead memories and broken hopes.

My pen was a part of the story and also was my silent friend who decided to stand by my side, helping me out to release my pain on paper when it was needed and providing some relief for the oncoming pain. My life was like a storybook that had glass pages made from solid tears using indelible ink. Freedom was my bed of dreams, which I used to sleep on at night, throwing my head on a wet pillow, fed and watered by my tears and growing every day in my garden of life. I'd always wished that my heart was strong enough to resist, before it had to fall apart and ask my absent strength for help. It wasn't easy for me, seeing my heart and my feelings in a permanent battle together, trying to appeal for a little mercy.

But when I lost the battle of cutting myself loose and I

announced the surrender, my pen stepped in quickly and we decided to write…

My pen was struggling to start the story and the way it felt to be a victim. It's very hard to tell the story and the way it turned out, but what I was sure about were the memories and the scars I had engraved in the back of my heart, and in my mind they were always ready to tell it the way it happened.

I was 12 years old, a good-hearted little child, who loved the colour of life. Painting and drawing birds on the school sketching board was my favourite hobby. I used to draw flying birds with big wings surrounded by green trees, the sky and moon and all sorts of views of nature. I had no idea that life would draw me a future painting and I would turn up and become one of those jailed birds, who always dreamed of cutting himself loose and enjoying the taste of freedom, or that I would just become a victim of a psychological hunter.

But life had decided already to provide me with variety of different sketches and here was my first sketch that was drawn by life at that time and not by me.

Plot

I was raised and spoiled by my mother, Ally was my father. We lived in a small flat, in a decent neighbourhood, in the capital city.

Alfred was my elder brother. My mother used to take care of me more than my older brother, as I was the youngest. She enrolled me in one of the best private language schools in the city, with a private driver, as I was very special to her. She used to spoil me and get me everything I wanted. On the other side, my brother Alfred was more attached to my father, as he was a troublemaker in school and in our neighbourhood was well known as a dangerous boy.

Alfred was pretty much like my dad, in terms of skin colour, mentality, manners, thoughts and everything else. My dad used to love Alfred more than anything in the world and used to spoil him and support him in any decision he made, whether it was wrong or right, and he also got him anything he wished for. But besides Alfred, my dad was a very stingy person regarding money with everyone else. During my childhood I used to see my father and mum fight a lot, and I grew up with the sound of my mum crying on a daily basis before she slept.

She used to get violently beaten up, regularly by my dad, till it ended tragically. Every morning I used to see a different type of bruise on her face. He was shouting and yelling at her almost non-stop, every single day. She was a victim of domestic violence and she was falling apart daily and felt hopeless.

All the neighbours felt sympathy for her and asked her why she stayed and endured all of that, as it was happening continuously!

I used to hear her screams behind her bedroom door and that used to scare me to death, but I couldn't help her as I was just a kid. My father also banned her from being in touch with her brothers and sisters, or any members of her family. My dad got Alfred to watch and spy on her, and report to him everything she did and every move she made; they both were against her.

My dad managed to poison Alfred's mind and convince him that she was an ungrateful and unfaithful woman and deserve it all. Alfred used to follow his orders just to satisfy him, with no consideration as to whether my father was right or wrong.

Years went by and I turned nine years old and that was the end of it, but I didn't see it coming that quick. She couldn't resist any more and she had given up. In fact she was a hero to have stayed all that time without falling apart, if she'd been a piece of stone she would have turned into ashes by now.

That was the only nine years of my life that I saw and lived with my mother. I was that kid in school who wished and hoped to have a normal life with a normal family, just like other kids. My heart and eyes were too young to have space for sadness or blues at that time, but that did not last for long.

In late summer 1992 I was doing the final school examination in primary school. It was a sunny and bright day. I finished the exam and all the kids were playing and were excited, as next day would be the big summer holiday. They ran back to their homes to celebrate and say goodbye to grade A.

Except me. I was standing outside school waiting for my driver to pick me up as usual, but he did not show up and I waited for more than an hour. I didn't know that that day I was waiting for my destiny to come and drive me off to different routes and a different destination. Beside the fact that life was preparing the party for the end of my childhood, hiding from me was a different kind of surprise.

Suddenly I saw my father approaching me and I remember his face wasn't normal, it seemed like something wrong had happened and he was ready to tell me bad news.

He said to me, "Sorry, your driver won't be able to come and pick you any more and that's why I am here today, to pick you up."

It didn't feel right at that moment and I knew out there something bad had happened, hidden behind his words, as a few seconds later he gave me some chocolate and I had never got sweets or candy from him before.

Then we walked together to his car and as soon as we reached it he looked at me and said, "Your mum has gone."

I did not understand what he meant by that but it wasn't convincing, as she had never complained about any sickness or ill health. I didn't say anything in the car and when we reached home I ran to my room and started to paint. There the bells of fear started to ring and I didn't know what was hidden from me in the woods. But the one thing I had to realize, or deal with, was the fact that next morning I wouldn't have my mother in the kitchen preparing my warm cup of milk.

I tried to convince myself that she was away for a couple of days, this was just a bad dream and things would get back to normal soon, but I never heard from her. Clearly I was trying to lie to myself. She never did come back.

So I lived the rest of my childhood with a question in my mind that had no answer: Where had my mother gone?

My father raised Alfred and I. My father was quite a high-ranking undercover detective in a secret police department. Alfred took himself aside and locked himself up in his room for three years. The only thing he did was study and he transformed from a bully and violent boy, into a nerd. It was very clear that he found this was the only way to escape and take revenge, considering the new environment we were facing. Quickly he became a very successful student in high school at that time.

With me things went in the totally opposite way. I transformed from a young, nerdy boy into a street kid, walking around randomly and seeking cigarettes to smoke.

My father loved Alfred a lot and they were too close to each other. Alfred hadn't been that close to my mother, as I had been. Being brought up by my mother, to them made me guilty, because I was my mother's boy and that's the crime I'd committed. The boy who was raised and spoiled by his mother was guilty and this was the reason for me to be punished with all kinds of illegal weapons and child cruelty. All the pain I started to suffer in my life and all the things that happened to me were just because I was too close to her and I was a double of, her face, her skin colour, her mannerisms and I even had the same smile.

My father changed my private school to a government school of course, to save money and to show me the real world. The government school was like my first day in a jail. My long blonde, fancy hair was sheared by scissors, as he knew that I always got attention from girls because of my hair and I remember that day because I locked myself in my room for three months until my hair had grown again.

He knew how sensitive I was and how quickly I got emotional and those were the cards he played to destroy all my senses. My clothes were confiscated and burnt in the middle of our living room, in front of my eyes; a few seconds later everything was turned to ashes. I was beaten and slapped on my face a thousand times every single day, with no mercy, in front of everyone and especially in front of the girls in our street that I used to love and hang out with, such as neighbours, or classmates. I had to eat completely rotten food, just because I forgot to put it in the fridge and to save money, as a part of his cruel plan to destroy my decency and innocence. I was the child who was not allowed to sleep and had to stand in front of him, watching him when he was eating, questioning me about what I done during the day and throwing food in my face. I would also get beaten if my eyes drooped to a wink or I fell asleep when I was talking to him.

I remember once, he came home from work, woke me up and questioned me at around 3:00 a.m., telling me, "If your brother was awake from now till tomorrow I would let you go sleep."

It was like a dirty game. How would Alfred wake up when he had just fallen asleep two hours earlier? The possibility of him waking up was at least six hours away. Imagine you have water in the desert and your son is asking you for some. You tell him if someone walks by, you will let him drink some water, but it is impossible to find someone walking in the desert, unless it is a miracle. I was dreaming and praying to God silently to make my brother wake up in the middle of the night, to drink some water, or go to the toilet, just to allow my father to let me sleep.

A few hours later, Alfred woke up around 5:30 a.m. and said to him, "Why are you still making him stand all day long? Give him a break and let him go to sleep."

That was a clear message to me that Alfred knew that I was being put on a cruel programme, just because I looked like my mother. And next morning, while I was sleeping, I got beaten and woken up with a shock, wondering what I had done.

Wishing for death was one of my dreams, which I struggled to achieve. Even the girl next door, who I used to love, witnessed me in action when I was falling apart. She also saw me entirely naked in the street, when my father decided to prevent me from wearing all the clothes I had on, stating that he owned them. I resisted so hard on the staircase, as we were living on the third floor, but he violently pushed me with his feet and kicked me until I reached the street. I was begging him to not do this to me in front of her and all my neighbours. I was a naked victim, beaten and crying, in the middle of a residential area on Main Street, seeing my love and other people in their flat windows watching a violent show and me covering my naked parts with my hands, while I was full of tears.

I won't also deny that while I am writing these words now I can't hold back my tears and I can't believe that it happened to me. That day I was broken-hearted and a broken human, and I decided to commit suicide and get rid of myself. I was ten years old when that happened and that was the first and deepest scar that was hammered into my memory and added to my collection, which time, days or even years would never erase from my mind. If I'd known, I would have wished to be dead before I stood in the street in public, naked and ruined like an animal. I remember she was crying and she acted like she didn't know me and shut her window. And that was the result that my father had been trying to achieve. I have seen all sorts of hell, physically and mentally, by my father's hand. I always wondered what I had done to be a victim and be guilty of something I wasn't a part of. My only crime was that I just looked like someone else he hated. So the only way to escape from all this was death.

I went to the local pharmacy to get sleeping pills, so I could have them all in one go, so I wouldn't feel any pain, as I was looking for the easiest form of suicide. But the pharmacist laughed at me and advised me to go home and drink some milk. I felt so offended and I walked away. I walked across the road to a different pharmacy and the pharmacist ran after me and held me by my arms, asking me to give him the telephone number of my family, so he could tell them. I ran away and failed to get the pills that would have ended my miserable life. I just decided to endure the pain and I carried on.

I went to a local government school, my father having enrolled me, where the education was underdeveloped. My grades went down from 95% to 63% in the first year. I hung out with the wrong schoolmates, fought and smoked cigarettes from pots in the street. We bullied young kids and stole their sandwiches. I ate unhealthy food and skipped classes, joining the school gang. My lifestyle dropped dramatically downwards, like angry storm. For three years I used sleep daily on a wet pillow that was fed by my tears, waking up by being beaten and shouted and sworn at, just like a slave. When I gave up on getting my life back, I made my way to the nearest local pharmacy again, asking the doctor there for suicide pills so I could sleep in peace, but the doctor kicked me out. I tried again, over and over, but it didn't work out, so I had to walk away and cut myself loose.

First I used to spend all day out, slumming around with street boys and at night I'd go back and crash in my father's car, which was parked just down from our house. I lived in the car for quite a long while, until the neighbours saw me in the morning when they went off to work. They told him there was some movement happening in his car during the night, in fear of someone stealing it. But in fact it was me who was stealing some sleep and rest before the sunrise, and the start to my day walking around randomly looking for a place to waste my time and a bit of food. I also remember I used to jump from our neighbour's house into ours, to steal some food, eat and shower, and change my clothes, leaving before the time he got home. When my father realized that I was sleeping in the car the next day the car was moved away and the only option I had at the time was to call my youngest uncle, Tami, who was a student of law in the University of Cairo. He was also living on a small amount of money he got from my father every month, as support. Tami lived quite far from our place. I walked all the way along to his place and that took me almost five hours to get there. When I knocked on his door he realized straight away that I had been kicked out and was looking for a place to sleep, as I had nowhere else to go.

He was happy to have me at the beginning, for the first few days, and then his friends started to come over to party at his place, smoking cigarettes and so on. Not long after he started to change, as he felt kind of tied down by having me around all the time, so he couldn't enjoy life fully. His friends were older than I was and they didn't particularly like having a little, sad kid in the place where they partied. He also wanted his life to be discreet and to keep his privacy, enjoying his younger years with no drama.

So after the first fight between him and me, I walked away for another five hours again, back to the car. I was crying all through the journey and suffered silently in pain, looking around me at a world that was not welcoming me at all. My broken dignity was complaining and wishing for death, as I felt totally unwanted. While I was walking this long distance, I felt that the people who were passing by, when they looked at me, they knew my story and they would feel sorry for me, and I hoped one of them would approach and cuddle me. I was the kid who was walking for hours on the streets, all through the night, his eyes completely wet with tears, nursing an empty stomach, looking and seeking a benefactor to adopt me and my broken life.

Of course I hadn't attended school for ages, as I was already busy with my new homeless lifestyle. So I went school and started to look for someone who was nerdy enough to teach me quickly a few words before the exams, so that I could just reach a PASS mark. I cheated and copied answers from the students who were seated next to me. Of course they had to let me do so, otherwise they would have to face the fact that after school they would be beaten up and that was the way it worked in government schools at that time. Here are the results of the three years in preparatory school: the first year score was 63 per cent. Second year score was 56 per cent. Third and final year was 67 per cent. So my score went from 95 per cent over five years in total, dropping off suddenly to average 55 per cent. To join the lowest university in Cairo you need at least 80 per cent in total over a three-year high school period to enter a law or economic university.

In Egypt it is considered hugely shameful for families if they have kids who can't score enough to get into university. It means the parents aren't good enough to educate their children properly in terms of manners, education, courtesy, etc. I had to face my father and tell him the result of my high school degree. My feet felt like they were shaking off with fear. Every minute that passed until he came back from work were the longest minutes of my life. I felt like a lamb waiting to be eaten by a lion, that I was waiting to say goodbye to life and would reach my grave when he returned home.

My father beat me until I was close to death that day. Neighbours knocked on our doors, appealing to him to leave me alone as I was screaming heavily, because he was beating me with a rubber water hose. He didn't allow for justice, fairness, or mercy in his judgment and didn't think that my result in high school was to be expected from a nine-year-old child, left alone with no care and no mother. He was thinking only about himself and how he was going to face people when they asked him which college Oscar was entitled to enrol in. I had only one option, which was private, expensive school.

But he had a different option which didn't exist on my agenda. So in order to get his revenge on me, as he thought that I had brought him shame, he decided to keep me at home with restrictive rules.

My clothes were locked up so I couldn't go anywhere. There was no going out, no phone, no TV, no radio and no friends. I wasn't allowed to do anything except study and repeat the last year of high school again, otherwise I would be out on the street for good. And he thought this was the way to get me to score 90 per cent to join a government university. Well, I started to smoke cigarettes and for the first time ever I spent my day watching TV for almost a year. Before he came back to the house I used to act like I was studying.

I had quite a bad experience with maths, as it's very obvious that maths needs to be explained by a teacher, but in my case as I was learning alone at home. My first big problem was with Pythagorean theorem. I guess if Pythagoras had been alive and knew that I would almost lose one of my eyes because of his theory, he wouldn't have even discovered it.

In order to understand this mathematics without going to school, a student would normally go for private lessons, but it was quite expensive at the time. So my dad, as punishment, decided to read the maths himself and explain it to me in his own way. The reason for that was of course to save money, or to be honest, he wouldn't spend money on someone like me. He had to teach me the theory by beating me on the back of my head and slapping me suddenly while I was looking at the book (for not understanding his way of teaching) and he claimed that I was mentally stupid.

So after six hours of crying next to him, trying to understand the theory, he beat me hard all of a sudden, without me expecting it. Of course, for me to prevent being hurt I put my hand in front of my face to avoid the beating, but my pen was still in my hand. He slapped me hard on my face and pushed the pen I was holding in my hand into my eye and it went through my skin just under the right eye by about a centimetre.

Pythagorean theorem was covered all over with my blood and the mathematics book was completely doused red.

He was surprised and shocked and he stood up and started screaming, beating his head into the wall and calling my brother from the other room.

"Come, please come take him away or go to hospital, as I am going to kill him and I'll end up in a jail."

He also was unconsciously talking to himself, saying that because of her, he was going to kill me.

From the opposite view, our neighbours were seeing an incident every day happening to me and everyone wished to take me away from him before I got killed, but no one dared to take this step. I wasn't sure who to blame, my father or Pythagoras! Or life! I was the victim of Pythagorean theorem. I lived with physical and mental pain every day for years.

One of our neighbours, who lived nearby, had just come back from Saudi Arabia. A family with a good boy the same age as me, named Mustafa. They were quite wealthy too and a few days after their arrival they were already witnessing some of the shows involving my pain and my story had already been told by other neighbours.

Mustafa felt sorry for me and tried to get close to me, but his family warned him not to be friends with me, to prevent any problems with my father. Mustafa bravely decided to take the risk and became a close friend of mine in a short time. He felt pity for me, as he was a witness to the hell I was living in, and he always wanted to help me out. Mustafa was very Western and the most fashionable boy in the area. He used to be very generous with me all the time, giving me fashionable clothes, perfumes, gifts, wallets, hair cream and fancy watches too. He also used to pay for me a lot when we used to go out and invited me if there were any special occasions.

I decided to find a job and earn money myself, so I could invite him back, as my dignity couldn't handle more help from people. There was a local souvenir shop in a quite posh area just around the corner from us. Three colleges surrounded this shop. The owner saw me as a good-looking little boy and that I could be perfect for the job, selling teddy bears, CDs, perfumes and all types of birthday cards and gifts. Mustafa gave me stylish clothes for that time; skinny jeans had just come out, along with Fila brand shoes and slim shirts.

At lunchtime I used walk around the area, as I had no money or food. I'd go back to the shop and the owner used to ask me, "Oscar have you eaten well? We have all day long!"

I used to tell him that I was full and my stomach blamed me for lying.

One day the owner said to me, "Oscar go for your lunch now, as we might get busy during the night." I usually walked out of the shop wondering where I might go, but this time I saw my father pulling in, in front of me!

He asked me where I'd got the clothes from and I said to him that they belonged to a friend of mine.

I was cornered between the car and the basement, and everyone, each group getting out the colleges, was looking at someone screaming and undressing a boy. I was crying and holding on hard to my trousers and the owner stepped out of his shop and told him leave me alone! That I was only a kid.

My father said to him, "This is my son and I'm allowed to do whatever I want."

By coincidence, my brother had just finished at his college and was walking by with his friends and he spotted a fight in the street where loads of people were gathered. He saw my father and me were screaming. He walked past very quickly, knocked me to the floor and started to beat me up, saying that I brought them shame everywhere I went.

Being alive was the reason for my pain. I was the kid who was taught to fear the dark, loneliness, even happiness. I used to fear the feeling of happiness, as I was always sure it would be temporary, that I had never even had it for a few seconds. I used to ask myself why it was happening to me. Why had life chosen me to be the victim? Why had I become a criminal of a crime which I had not committed?

Until the day came when I heard my brother asking my father, "Why? Why are we doing this to him? You know he did not do anything and he is just a kid."

My father said to him, "I don't know. When I look at him I just feel disgusted. I guess because his face reminds me of his mother's, he's just got her face, her eyes, smile, skin, voice, laugh, everything. When I look at him I just remember her and I feel I just want to kill him for revenge."

That night I was half asleep and I was scared to death, I couldn't hold back my tears. My eyes started to shed waves of tears that would fill a river and I realized, when the sun rose, that I should be out looking for shelter, as that would be the end of it. I decided to walk away... no matter where was I going to stay, or how I was going to eat, sleep, or even survive.

I'd been wishing for death every day of my life since my mother had gone. But at that time, I didn't care what would happen, my heart was begging me to run away and escape. I had nothing to lose and I was lost already. What would I stay for? So I made up my mind and I decided to leave for good.

That day I walked around the area randomly and met a street gang. They offered to spend time with me and the first thing they presented to me was a marijuana cigarette.

As soon as I put it in my mouth I ended up coughing myself to death and I threw up. I got high and I remember I was crying and laughing at the same time, followed by me vomiting in a dark corner off the street. Someone in the gang felt guilty and sorry for me. He said to them that he wasn't going to allow this to happen and let me get as lost as he was. I didn't look like them. He took me aside and told me to run away and not to return back there again.

I hid again and as soon as the sun came up I went back to our flat. I had to jump from our neighbour's window into ours and lied, saying to my neighbours I'd forgotten my keys, so things could still look okay. I went to the kitchen and had a meal and I remembered that my father owned another flat in a quite faraway place. I stole the keys, clothes, food, kitchen tools, plates, glasses, kettle etc. and I set off carrying all my personal stuff in a big black rubbish bag and in the other hand, I carried my broken heart and my suicide dream in another bag.

I walked for more than four hours outside of town, to the area where the flat was. The flat was only just finished and the area was still under construction, as it used to be a part of the desert and the government had decided to spend money and develop the area. The streets were dark and dangerous. There weren't any shops around. The streets were only full of slumdogs and labourers that worked in construction, who came from all over the countryside seeking jobs in Cairo.

The journey of fear started. I used to stay up all the night, as I was scared. I made friends with one of the shops that was a 24-hour off-licence, called Linacre, just to keep me company overnight till the sunrise, so I could go to sleep. He used to offer me food too and a cigarette, as he was always feeling sorry for me, but he was a simple guy and all he could offer was just some biscuits and crisps. I had to walk four hours every day to reach my original area, just to meet any one of my neighbours, so I could talk to someone and get one of them to give me a pound to get something to eat.

I considered myself dead, while still breathing in the meantime. Now when I remember this time I feel speechless and my heart stops, as I wonder how and where I got the strength to manage to walk the streets looking for a benefactor who had a tissue to dry my shedding tears and save my young dreams from suicide. There was no big difference between the dogs and I. The only difference was that they didn't need to worry about feeding those without dignity.

One day I fell and I was almost dying, as my body contained no protein or muscle. When Karl saw me falling apart because of illness, he decided to make a move and get help. Karl was a friend of mine, who was a big fan of my character and he used to admire the way I expressed my pain. He was also from a broken family, but a fresh victim still and his mother looked after him along with his sister too. Karl called Tim (my youngest uncle) and begged him to call up one of my rich uncles who lived abroad.

He said to Tim that, "Oscar is seriously sick and his body is losing blood, he has no protein and needs immediate help."

Tim chose to contact my Uncle Han who lived in Namibia, as he was teaching science in a college there and he was the only one who used to love me as his own son.

My Uncle Han flew quickly to Cairo, saw that I was ill in bed and that I couldn't move. He gave Karl money to buy a mobile phone for me, so he could contact and keep in touch with me after he left to go back to Namibia. He also left a decent amount of money and asked Karl to stay with me and cook and look after me, which he would pay him for. But Karl refused to take the money. My uncle decided to pay for me to join the most expensive private high school in Cairo and to be completely responsible for all my expenses.

It was a rescue mission for him, to save me from being lost, a drug addict, in a street gang, or dead on a street corner. He decided to open the cage and free my dreams, which had been behind bars for ages, hoping the day would come and they would run away.

I start to recover slightly. Karl stayed for quite a while. We used to share the same cigarette and eat the same food, and I started to write and write, over and over, telling Karl about my dreams.

And that was the first time I started to write, when my pencil refused to paint or draw any more.

And here is the first thing I ever wrote:

The Funeral Of My Dreams

I remember I was there when the night always used to be there for me to serve my wounds.

I was there when my tears struck and declined to contribute.

I was there when I had to call all my wounds for an urgent meeting, as I was invited to attend my own funeral in the court of life.

I was there when my feelings refused to attend and were resisting.

I was there when my emotions protested and asked for another appeal.

I was there when my broken heart resisted and asked my mind for help.

I was there when I witnessed where my dreams were executed and buried.

I was there when I saw my words commit suicide in the library of reality.

I was there when I witnessed the waves of my blues being taken away and were rested in the ocean of life.

I was escorted by a bleeding heart to the grave, under the secret force of happiness.

I was there and witnessed the pain feeding my tears, growing up in my garden of life.

I was a patient in life's hospital and my broken strength was my nurse.

I was a student who was expelled from the school of life.

These were the first words that came out on paper when I started to write, when I was around 15 years old. Karl that day bought a bottle of vodka and started to drink and drink. I asked him what he thought about my writing! He read it and he started to cry.

He was totally boozed up with alcohol and shouting loudly he said, "No one would read our words. No one would listen to our voice. No one would feel for us, we are the living dead. We are going to die here Oscar."

He was screaming all over the place. He was feeling sorry for me and exploded for me, as he was amazed by my silence. I believed every word he said and I start to drink myself, throwing vodka on my agenda where my words were written. And then I set it on fire.

Personally, I would never forget that day in my life.

Karl's family started to feel worried and asked for him to go back home. He promised me as soon as he got chance he would escape and buy cigarettes, and come to see me. He told me to keep going and be strong.

When I ran out of food and cigarettes I called Mustafa and told him where I was living now. Mustafa brought me a Walkman, as he knew I loved music. I couldn't afford to buy a daily battery for it so I had to buy an adaptor, but it was the only entertainment I had. He also got me a few things to help me survive for a bit. Mustafa started to come and visit me a lot. He took me out to see the world and to introduce me to his friends. In a short time Mustafa got busy with his school and his family. One of the posh groups of friends he'd introduced me to, lived close to me and they became my best friends. Their families were so rich, living in America and other countries, sending ridiculous amounts of money to them every month and they lived in villas and drove Porsche cars. They had everything anyone dreams of; expensive cars, knew beautiful girls, ate classy food, a completely different lifestyle to the one I was used to.

The place ended up being called the Vegas of Cairo city. Quickly I became their master and the most beloved and funny person ever, keeping their secrets and advising them. Simply, I was the person who they could trust and listen to. They had the money, but they needed the right person to guide them with how and where to spend it, and most importantly, how to enjoy it! They relied on me for everything; where to go and what to do, every day. We used to share girls, laugh, joke, play, travel, race and even fight. I was their leader and everything to them.

All of a sudden I was turned into a totally different person, I had new clothes, was driving my friends' luxurious cars, had crashes and went to parties in their houses. We did everything recklessly. I had anything I wanted. I knew how to dress, how to impress, how to talk. I was so classy in the way I treated women, the way I drove their cars, the way I acted. I was almost living a celebrity lifestyle.

After a year's intermission, I wondered who would get my life in order. The answer was no one, it was all about me. I was in control. I decided to leave and make my own life. I had forgotten that I was enrolled in the poshest private language school in Cairo, the most special of high schools, the only mixed school of exceptional boys and girls who were the kids of celebrities and politicians in Egypt.

I made my way to the school and I realized that I had skipped the first year already. When the people of my age were learning in school about maths, history, geography, politics, etc. I had been living and engaged in my own school, so I missed a lot of formal education. But while they were studying what people had written in books, I was practising it for real, through action.

I had too many friends who passed through my life. One of them set me up with his girlfriend's best friend and she was called Wisam. She was young and pretty, had long hair and a perfect body. We dated a lot. I used to impress any girl I met with the most classy and expensive places; hotels, coffee shops and all the romantic, posh spots in Cairo and I was generously spending money too.

After few month of dating I was dumped and I was kind of broken. I would listen to sad and sorrowful music 24/7 and would wonder why she had done this to me, until I met one of her close friends. I confronted her and I asked her why Wisam had dumped me.

"What did I do? What I have done wrong! Please help me I'm broken!"

She was embarrassed and her face acted funny, like she was hiding something. Then she looked at me and said, "Oscar, have you ever considered touching her?"

I asked her what she meant.

She said, "This is weird to say Oscar, but Wisam expected more from you than just romantic love, talking and going out."

I understood why I had been dumped then. I was shocked. I was broken. My image of treating girls had changed entirely and I decided to get revenge for my broken heart. The same night I called Wisam up and I told her I wanted to speak with her urgently. We met and then we kissed. We started to touch each other in the taxi, on the bus and even on the train. We needed more privacy as we were desperate! We planned to catch up the day after, but this time at my place. We made love and I remember it was kind of intense.

Unconsciously, while we were in the middle of making love, she held me hard by my neck and said to me, "You are incredible. If you dump me I will kill you."

The day after we had sex again at my place, at her place, basically every place! I wanted to prove to her that I could be the person she wanted. Then a few weeks later, Wisam was indeed dumped.

She cried like hell. She believed that I'd broken her heart, but the reality was she'd broken mine. She started chasing me everywhere; by phone, at home, at the places I used to spend time. But I was done. I was just having different thoughts about love. I had a respect for girls, but she'd erased that terribly and had taken that away. Loving her or love in general, for me, was about: feelings, emotions, respect, hopes, innocent dreams, sacrifices, or sharing feelings in love letters with a red heart at the top, or perhaps some red lipstick kisses on a white tissue. But all that changed and I was bellowing away that this was just the beginning for the new Oscar.

The Greatest Change

Here was my first adventure, when I acted in my life with no principles. One day I had a call from one of my wilder friends. He phoned me and invited me to his house, as he had a prostitute at his place! Going by my conversation with him a few days earlier, I had broken up with my girlfriend, I was willing to change and I was ready for a new adventure and to become a playboy. The party was on. I phoned three other friends and we headed off in my friend's car, driving along to our other friend's house where the girl was.

We parked the car in front of the building's entrance and we took the stairs to the second floor, all discreetly of course, as the neighbours would involve the police if we got caught.

Hassam was in the living room waiting for us. We asked him where the girl was and he told us that she was naked in the bedroom waiting for one of us and that we would go in one by one! Everyone was so scared and shaking. Hassam started to push everyone to get in the room and no one want to go.

Nageb suggested, "Let's all of us go in, in one go."

The girl was lying down on the bed and when she saw four more guys walk in the room, she stood up and said, "What the hell do you guys think you're doing! Only one person stays. I am not a minibus here, I am a human being and can't take all of you in one go." She said Google and porn websites had nothing to do with reality.

Someone said, "Okay, one will go and the rest will watch!"

She started to laugh and said, "You guys are funny."

We all got naked and waited for our turn, but suddenly we heard the sound of the door and someone trying to open it using a key.

Hassam was shocked and said, "Shit, shit, shit. My family have just come back." He pulled the girl by her hair and hid her behind the door.

His father walked in and saw Hassam naked with four other nude guys around him. He was even more shocked and suddenly pulled his hair, screaming, "No way, my son is gay!"

While we stood behind him, Hassam replied, "No Dad, your son is innocent. A girl is here," and he got the girl out from behind the door.

His father put his hand on his heart and walked out of the room. We slowly started to look around and ran towards the living room exit, but we found his father coming our way with a mop handle held aggressively in his hand. We ran as quickly as we could, all of us naked, towards the car, going fast where we could and carefully where we had to, until we reached the main entrance with the car parked out in front. I opened the central locking with the car keys from inside the hallway and we walked, all four of us entirely naked, to the car.

While I started the engine there was screaming from Hassam's flat. We could hear, "Enough, enough! We didn't even sleep with her."

One of the resident families was taking fresh air and a cup of tea on the balcony. They saw us, but couldn't say anything, as they were staring at us and couldn't believe what they were seeing. I drove away very fast and my two friends seated in the back hid from public view, along with my other friend who was next to me, but unfortunately, as I was driving, I could not get myself covered at all. The only thing I managed to do was to put my right hand on the steering wheel and had my left hand covering my sensitive parts.

I called a friend and told him that I was making my way to his place. "Please open your garage when I reach you and have four sets of pants with you!"

He thought I was joking, but in fact I was not. I can't stop thinking, when I look back, what people's impressions must have been in such an Islamic culture, as they were at the bus stop waiting for the bus and they saw four naked guys driving by.

This was my first adventure in my world of freedom.

School & Education

I went back to school as a different person, repeating the first year of high school, making friends, a reputation and a new legend for myself everywhere. Across the road from my classy school was another French school, called the Lycée Français. This French school was the competitor to ours.

British, American and French students attended there and I had a big fight with the boys from the Lycée Français. A war started between both schools and expensive cars were damaged because of rocks that were thrown. The police came and picked up people from both sides, with me staying five hours in a cell.

One of my secret fans showed up at the police station, his father paying my bail so I could go home. This boy was named Mahmoud Race, as he was a famous bike racer. His father was a high-level manager in Lufthansa airlines and British Airways. I was out in a few hours, his father telling me to stay out of trouble. Then Mahmoud introduced himself to me and said what a big fan he was of my popularity in school.

When I got back to school the day after, I was in control. I was famous and a bully boy, but in a way that served justice, protecting the school from intruders, or strangers, standing and protecting the naïve boys. I had attention from all the girls in school. The school turned into my kingdom. I used to walk around with a bunch of bully boys; they were my army and I was their leader.

Mahmoud was ridiculously rich, but he was lonely with no friends and single, of course. He had no experience of anything in life expect his beloved, speedy bikes. Mahmoud was the only rich, young boy in Egypt who drove a £40,000 bike, which came as a special order from Japan. He was a target and a good catch for a thief. He loved me a lot and I considered him my younger brother. He gave me loads of money, which even the rich families didn't have. He gave me a mobile phone as a gift, at a time when mobile phones were just out. He taught me how to drive super racing bikes and showed me a different world. We became like twins in a very short time.

I taught him how to dress, to love, to smile, to speak, to communicate, how to think and how to be brave. Basically, I taught him everything I knew and about every experience I had learnt. I was like a hero to Mahmoud; I was his role model and his legend.

He told his parents that, "Oscar is a treasure and I have discovered him. I am going to leave and stay with him."

His parents hated me a lot, just as Karl's and Mustafa's had. They always thought that I was taking their kids away from them at such a young age. Mahmoud refurbished my dirty flat and provided a computer and all the fancy living accessories. Computers at that time were only in government offices. No one had a computer, as it cost £6,000 in 2002.

I visited Karl and he was so happy to see me. I had to pay him back for helping me, when he had nothing. I introduced him to Mahmoud and we started to share everything again. Mahmoud was always jealous of my other friends, as he wanted to be the closest and nearest person to the legend that I'd become, so they never liked each other. But I am not just talking about Karl and Mahmoud, all my friends fought and challenged each other to be the one dearest to me.

I set Mahmoud up with a supermodel girl and we started a new journey, beautiful girls, racing bikes, cars and wealthy places; a super-rich lifestyle, going out and seeing the world in a way no one had seen it before. But I didn't know that the pain was still chasing me everywhere I went. It seemed like the pain was messing me around.

One day, on a summer's morning in Cairo, I was listening to music in Mahmoud's BMW and we were going to head off to get some food from McDonald's. At one of the traffic lights nearby, I suddenly saw my father's car pulling in front of me in the street.

He walked slowly towards me and looked me up and down, asking, "Whose car is this?" I was wearing a G-Shock watch, which was around £500 at that time. He also said, "Where did you get this watch?"

I was freaked out. I was getting ready to run with the car if he tried to beat me.

He carried on and said, "Do you sell drugs now or what? Where did you get all those things?"

I told him the items belonged to my best friend.

He said, "What kind of friend has got all of this money? And how can he leave these valuable cars and phones and watches with you, just like that?"

He did not believe me and thought I had become gay or was dealing drugs. It was hard for him to believe that the weak, feeble boy I once was, had grown into a fine young man.

All my fears and shyness were gone. I was smart and stylish too. I knew exactly what I needed to do, it wasn't writing, it wasn't books, it was much bigger than that. It was revenge. I was dating and having sex every single day with different girls. They were all calling me the hardest drug that anyone could ever quit.

I had everything they could dream of, money, cars, intelligence and a good sense of humour. I was stylish, sophisticated, classy, good-looking and experienced at such a young age. I was good at flirting and conversing. I was good at foreplay and making love. I was a treasure for all those girls. I was almost going to be in their dreams, on a white horse, just like all girls' fantasies, but I was in a white BMW instead.

During those years I did not see my brother for ages, I did not even know anything about him and I did not try to find out. But I heard he was travelling abroad, doing courses in human rights in Canada, France, Italy and finally he settled in England.

In a very short time I was well known in every single rich community, sports club and nightclub. I was considered very remarkable and unique.

Late in 2004, I was invited to a party on the first day of Eid. All my friends were there that day and there was alcohol, cars, bikes, phones, money and we were all staying in one of our friend's houses, celebrating the Eid and hoping and dreaming with joy, thinking about what Eid was bringing for us, just like Christmastime. But it was written for me to have different expectations! Eid was coming with the greatest surprise for me.

We were waiting for Mahmoud to join us. He was late, his phone was busy and a few hours later we'd started to get drunk. Then Mahmoud showed up and I wished he hadn't. He walked in the room and he was looking at me, and it seemed like he was hiding something.

I told him, "Say it! Say it! What's up? I have been calling you and your phone was busy for hours."

He said to me, "I was talking to your mother."

"Right! Nice joke. So what is the plan for tonight?"

He replied saying, "I am not joking Oscar. Someone just called me and she got my mobile number from the school. She is claiming to be your mother and she begged me to let her get in touch with you."

I was shocked. In fact shocked isn't the right word. I was speechless. No, I think even speechless isn't the right word to describe my feelings at that moment. But it felt like a bullet went through my heart and tears jumped from my eyes as if from a cliff.

All my friends, who I was surrounded by at this moment, didn't believe a word of it and one of them told Mood that it wasn't a good joke, as he was ruining our night. My friends said they had known me for years and were under the impression that my mother was dead.

Mood said, "Well anyway, she will call in a few minutes and you will find out."

I remember my heart was beating slowly and loudly. I could barely remember her voice, or how she looked, to be able to confirm whether she was really my mother or not.

The phone rang and I heard someone crying and saying, "Oh baby, forgive me for leaving you alone all those years, but I had no choice. I am your mother. I have been dreaming of the day that I would find you and the chance to be able to tell you that I am sorry and that I love you, before I died. Please let me see you now."

I did not say anything. Eventually I agreed and said, "Okay, let's meet up in a place you want."

It was 3:00 in the morning and all my friends were worried that it could be a trap, or a joke, so they decided to sprint around the place we were going to meet and pretend they were just normal people.

I was driven by Mahmoud and behind us were three cars guarding us as a backup. We went, as requested, to a big square. No one was there except a white car with an old man and an old woman in the passenger seat, with a child on her lap.

I heard the old man saying to her, "Yes, here he is. Is this your son? Go and take your son in your arms."

She walked toward me slowly and then she hugged me with tears in her eyes saying, "Thank God I found you after all these years. Thanks to God. I was praying every day and asking God to help me find you."

I was silent. Looking around me, I saw my friends who were hiding and were crying and getting emotional.

She took me to the car and said, "This is my husband and this is my daughter."

I got into her car and sat in the back, heading to their place to sit together and talk. I remember looking behind me to make sure my friends were still with us and there for me.

She offered me food and her husband went to sleep, as he was ill and suffering from cancer. She explained to me what happened eight years ago when she disappeared. She explained how she suffered and how she wished for death every day during the time living with my dad, and that I was the only thing that made her hold on and endure the pain. She cried again and again, but something held my tongue from speaking.

Maybe my heart had become a piece of stone! Or maybe it was the opposite way around and my heart was too weak to handle the shock. Or maybe I just wanted to say silently that it was too late now! Where were you when I needed you? I just had no clue what to say. But I deeply believed that the pyramids of pain I had built up and the mountain of sadness which was inside me, quickly was becoming a volcanic temper that was falling apart.

A week later, she phoned me and she said that her husband had died. It was clear from the tremble in her voice that she was crying out for help. She wanted me to comfort her and consider starting a new life with her, just like the old days, but the old days were gone now. I offered her my condolences and said goodbye. I felt like such a coward, because I deserted her when she needed me most. But I just couldn't bring myself to help her when I was engulfed in my own mountain of misery. I felt as though happiness had been banned from my life and I was permanently a prisoner of my past.

I did not have a vision of the future, or any signs of light at the end of the tunnel, as English people say. So I decided to hide, so I didn't have to face the new facts and the bile of the remaining feelings that I had. I didn't want to talk to anyone or see anyone. I lived in the dark alone, listening to Era and Enigma tracks, and Buddha Bar secret love tracks sometimes. Until one day I went back to my usual area and I met some of the boys on the street talking about arranging to rob someone named Charley's mobile phone. He was looking to sell it to them, as they'd pretended that they had the money and would buy it from him, but the fact was that they'd decided to steal it and make a run for it.

I waited until the guy arrived then I took him away and told him that he was being set up and they would steal his expensive phone. He asked me for protection and I took him away in my friend's car and we invited him for dinner.

Charley and I became the strongest of friends after that, more like twins. He was a pharmacist and really wealthy, and that gave us a power to explode with confidence, as he had the money and I had the bright mind to spend it in the right places, redecorating our lives and ourselves. I taught him how to become sophisticated and enter the highest of class levels. I also taught him how to drive. I hooked him up with girls and we had too much fun. Everyone thought we were brothers as we had so many things in common. We were the perfect match; we had the same mentality, the same thoughts and were the same age.

Charley was very smart and was learning to become a professional with the information I had given him. He applied it quickly, until he became better than me. Charley wasn't only a best friend of mine; he was a friend, a brother, a father and guarded my life. He didn't allow anyone to hurt me any more and he wanted revenge on the people who'd wounded me. Charley offered to pay any price to clean up my past and let me be reborn with a new beginning. I won't forget, when Charley used to wake up in the morning, before I went to my exams, he'd give me the keys to his car and a £100 note, telling me keep them with me in case after my exam I wanted to buy something with my college mates. He had a big heart and was extremely loyal. Charley was my benefactor, who I'd met by chance, and he was trying to help me out burying my blues and starting a new life. He was so kind and sensible. He used to tell me to keep in touch with my mother and look after her baby as an escape. He used to buy toys and candies and give them to me when I went visit them three times a year.

I introduced Charley to all the contacts I knew and he did the same. All the people I knew used to hate Charley, as they considered him the thief who'd stolen the treasure from them.

My uncle came for a visit to check on me and he bought an expensive, luxurious flat in one of the skyscrapers and offered it to me, so I could leave the crappy one I lived in. He also paid for me to join the college I liked. I chose to study a BA in literature, as I used to be very good at philosophy. So after high school, I picked my university to be as far away from maths as possible, because of my past experience with Pythagorean theorem, which hadn't been too pleasant.

I moved to the flat with Charley and we were over the moon with our new lifestyle, the high level of luxury and the richest neighbourhood in the country. We started to make friends and we entered a life of drugs. Hash used to be the most expensive drug, as no one could afford it at that time. But the guys who smoked it had a different lifestyle compared to anyone else; a family living abroad and sending them money, or they were spoiled by their rich family.

Very quickly I was addicted to it and they named me Doctor Hash. I used to smoke huge amounts, the sort that could kill someone in a day. I couldn't drive without it! I couldn't do anything without it. It was the painkiller of my internal, mental pain. It was the permanent medicine I was looking for.

The strange part was when others used to smoke it recreationally, it worked for them, giving them a normal high and they would start to act in their own way. Some would laugh loudly, some would fight, some acted like animals, or got hungry or dirty. Some became extremely energetic and they would start to speed up their actions.

But for me, drugs worked differently. I felt I became more artistic doing things. I felt I got smarter and more conscious, sensible and visible. I was also, at that time, getting older and growing up. I had no energy any more to fight for my freedom. I had given up, was sick and tired, and finally fed up too.

I retired wiser and became an adviser in life matters: love, family, friends, sex, drugs, even in art. I was the man with taste. I was mainly silent all the time, but when I spoke, everyone enjoyed listening. The people who knew me used to say that I was like a friendly cancer; very effective, easily attacked your heart and body in seconds, took control and lead your emotions.

Girls used to describe me in too many different ways. They used to call me a drug that was hard to quit, because I had given my life to them and others. I was a teacher to them, and I was their painkiller and medicine for their wounds. I applied fairness and justice to every situation before I made any decision. I was their shelter and their tissue to dry their tears. My heart and my feelings were the guides that gave light to my mind before any judgment was made in my life, I never followed my mind. I was the person who kept their deepest secrets of girls and boys. I was their confusion priest. I was the church and the mosque and the court of justice for them.

I hadn't met my father for almost ten years and I had no idea about my brother, where he was, how he was doing, or even what he looked like!

I used to give my mother money when I visited her twice a year, but she wasn't in need of money, she wanted me to stay and I always left her in tears when she saw me going. I was scared that my father would know that I had found her.

My heart had been replaced with a piece of stone, or I felt old enough not to need a mother's love after what I had been through. I also wanted to head off towards my goal, to get revenge from poverty and the hunger that I had been through alone, with no support.

As my father reached a higher rank in the police department, he had an opportunity to recruit new officers and he offered me a position as a secret police detective, and as I'd always dreamt of being a police officer, I had to accept the job. In a very short time I was the youngest and smartest secret police detective that they had. Very quickly I became a person near the top of government; the person who had the biggest connections and relationships with all the authorities in the country, particularly the corrupt ones.

I was in power. I was limitless. I could issue a driving licence with a phone call. I could sort any problem, at any police station, just with a phone call. My playground was in jails and police stations; my fun was with IDs and issue permutations.

Charley followed in my steps wherever I went. Our nights were so long and never-ending. Every day we spent the night either at checkpoints at city borders, having a good time with police officers, or meeting the biggest and richest sharks that needed to escape the law to get their business done without paying tax. Charley got to know me so completely and he was the only person who could read my mind before I even spoke. Just by looking into my eyes he could know exactly what I was going to do next. We were so important and every day we were invited places by important people who wanted something from us.

We had seen a different part of life and living, money and dangers. We were heartless and brave. I made ridiculous amounts of money. We couldn't get along with normal people who were the same age as us. They were out of our league in psychological matters, smartness and thoughts, or even in the pain we had suffered. No one we ever met experienced pain as we did.

Principles & Dignity For Sale

There were times when I had to sell out my principles indeed.

This is can sound a bit weird, but it is kind of reality, as 90% of people who I've met since I was born are living now without any kind of principles, or even dignity.

Principles and dignity can be sold in too many different ways, like any other cheap item, but particularly they would be sold for specific reasons, or I personally call it, a package: sex, money, food, position, desire, benefits, acts, etc...

Principles can also be sold in two ways in our life, either by force, or through a person's perspective.

Sometimes you find a mother works as a prostitute in Soho, but for the sake of feeding her kids back home.

Sometimes you find a girl selling her body for the sake of getting a gift, such as a Louis Vuitton bag, or for a promotion at work, by sleeping with her line manager.

Sometimes you find a wife, or a husband, cheats after a number of years of marriage, just because they couldn't control their relationship when time pass them by and their marriage got boring.

In respect of money and sex, I would say not only can principles be sold, but also humans themselves can be sold. People must know that a human being with no dignity or morals won't have any purpose for living or existing and have no idea, in my personal opinion, as I personally believe that dignity and principles are human beings' value and the most valuable elements humans could ever have, which are also unique and priceless.

Personally, if I had to choose between living richly, but without dignity, or to die from poverty, but with dignity, I would rather die, no doubt. But in my case, I have already been dead, so I haven't too many options. I learnt the hard way that life is much stronger than us and it can bring us to our knees.

I remember when I was one of those kids who used have principles and rules to follow and respect in life; I was against people who smoked cigarettes and drugs. I used to hate people who smoked and damaged their health for no reason and wasted their money for nothing. But I've learnt now not to be judgmental, as I am now one of the heaviest smoking people ever.

Even drugs were a no-go area for me and I was a strong believer that drug dealers all must be discriminated against in public squares so they could suffer just as the drug addicts, who suffered every single moment from the poison they bought every single day. But again I was one of those victims and the choice was entirely mine when I became one of the drug dealer's slaves.

I sold my principles when I smoked drugs almost non-stop for five years continuously. I am sorry, but it was the only way to help my brain relax and give my mind a temporary break.

I also remember I was a strong believer that the definition of love is when your feelings control your heart and your entire mind.

I did sell my principles when I followed my new definition of love, using sexual elements to make girls weak and addicted, in the name of love.

I sold my principles when I helped all those who broke the rules and I kept silent and helped them.

Yes, I sold my principles when I became one of those drug dealer's victims.

Yes, I sold my principles when accepted fraudulent money to go into my back pocket.

Yes, I sold my principles when I allowed food to get into my stomach without knowing from where the money had come from.

Yes, I sold my principles every time I had sex with a girl without love or even knowing her name.

Yes, I sold my principles when I decided to sleep with one of the girls who I used to love, after she cheated on me.

Yes, I sold my principles when I saw wrong things happen in front of my eyes and I ignored it.

Yes, I sold my principles when I zipped my mouth shut and could not say no when I wanted to.

Yes, I sold my principles each time I smiled in someone's face that I did not like.

Yes, I sold my principles when I pretended I was happy and in fact I was not.

Yes, I sold my principles when I had to choose what made others happy and overwhelmed myself.

Yes, I sold my principles when I closed my eyes when I saw something wrong and just minded my own business.

Yes, I sold my principles when I realized that everything I had done was against my religion, personality and even my life's rules.

Yes I failed. I could not cope or live with the guilt of losing my values.

Yes I failed. I could not cope or live with the pyramids of pain I carried inside me.

Yes, I could not manage to live for long with all the bad things I had captured.

I even failed to heal the scars that had been drawn on my concrete heart.

Yes, I could not cope and live with that fact that I'd sold my dignity.

Yes, I used to believe that sometimes you had to get lost to find yourself, but I had given up the hope of being found.

The Great Resignation...

Here was the biggest escape plan. I had decided to bet again on the auction of life and buy back what I had lost, capturing again the missing parts. I was trying to gather my jigsaw puzzle life together. I started to go to my college and attend classes again, trying to cover what I had missed from my education. I was learning in the biggest school – real life – learning the hard way, but I was missing the academic part that was written in books.

I also changed my mobile number and I was slowly keeping a distance from anything that could drag me back to the person I was before.

But there were a few negative things that remained still, of course:

Yes, I could not quit smoking hash, as hash had become my mental health medicine.

Yes, I could not quit my charm skills of picking up the hard, pretty girls and making incredible love with them.

Yes, I could not stop flirting and using my own cheesy pickup lines.

So when I went back to college I tried to act like a normal student and get along with the regular college boys, but obviously they could still see the difference in my personality compared to any other schoolboys. They started to get attracted by my character, as I was very mature, stylish, smart and bright. They also noticed the way I talked and rolled, and so I started to select the super hot girls from amongst the crowds; they were easy fish for me and very decent compared with others.

So here was my relapse: I stayed almost five years in my uncle's luxurious flat, stoned non-stop, all day long, having sex every day with different types and characters of girls. I was in love with all of them. Each one of them had something I loved about them.

Jasmine used to look after me all the time. She was so simple and from a poor family. She cleaned my dishes and washed my clothes and changed my bed sheets. She knew that she was not the only girl I knew, but she was happy with it as I was more than her dream. Every time we met she kissed my hand and I hated it, and I always wanted to tell her that I was a very simple person, not a god.

Miro used to be the dreamy future girl, classy, sophisticated, cultured and from a big, respectable family. I always used to hurt her by saying you are my dream wife, but I can't afford to have someone like you, as I have no future.

Ammy was a crazy girl, who wanted to hang out, like other girls, with a celebrity lifestyle. I was too much for her too and I remember her parents got her engaged to one of her cousins. When I knew that she was still talking to me after she had got engaged, I refused to stay with her, as this was against my principles. We split up and a few months later she got married and named her son Oscar. She was nuts. She had short dark hair, wore men's perfumes, big Diesel watches, jeans and a black, slim leather jacket; she was also one of those Internet hackers. She was stylish, crazy, stubborn, loved adventures and fashion. She was a very difficult and smart girl.

I have to admit that not everybody could handle a girl with these types of qualities. It was not easy at all for me to get into her phone, as she used all types and kinds of passwords in order to make sure everyone wouldn't be able to access her phone. You basically would struggle to catch her if she was playing around or hiding something unfaithful. But all this technology couldn't stop me. I used all my smart skills to get her under control and when I got to the point when she was mine, she surrendered to my power, admired my brightness and she was mine, full-time on the phone and in the bedroom.

She was mental and she was my signature. We used all kinds of sex positions, normal ones, abnormal ones and even our own creations. We were like animals and we used to hurt each other physically. She used to love pain and that's the way she tasted the joys of life, or perhaps she was addicted to sex, but only with each other. We used to have sex every day for six to nine hours till we passed out, we'd wake up eat and do the same over and over. We had sex in the car, public toilets, parks, even in a hospital. We did it at my place, at her place, basically every place. She cut her wrist twice, using a knife at my place, when I decided more than once to break up with her.

Karl had grown up and started to follow Charley and me around, and he learnt everything in a very short time. I was his coach and his role model in life too. A while later I announced my retirement. My mobile number was changed and my car model and colour was also changed, and my uncle's new luxury penthouse was my hidden place. I cut my connections with all the people that I knew and the only two people who could reach me at that time were Charley and Karl, besides Ammy of course.

I told Charley that Karl had to be looked after, as he was still young and I didn't want him to enter the snake house as we had, as he wouldn't be smart enough to get himself out of it safely. We gave Karl our complete trust and money, let him drive our cars, and I also gave him some sex advice and a drugs lecture, so he could hunt for his own girl and not get addicted to drugs.

After I'd won the auction and I owned again all that I'd lost of my dignity and principles, I started to think a lot about the past, present and future, but what surprised me was how I'd ended up doing all this and how lucky it was that I was still alive and safe. I started to think about God, as he was the only one who could help me, in fairness.

At this point I started, for the first time in my life, to try to pray and introduce myself to God, but it didn't last long. I started to smoke again heavily, plus I had my sex addiction with Ammy. There was a strange feeling – that almost controlled my mind and my heart – that something bad would happen to me. I started to picture the way I was going to die. It always came to my mind in two forms, a car accident, or burned in an exploding car crash. I was so scared of death, as I didn't want to die with shame, guilt and sins. I'd done everything wrong and forbidden in life, except betray a friend of mine.

Everyone started to notice that I'd begun to have a phobia about death. It was rare that I would decide to go out at night for a spin, as I never wanted to leave my room at all and I wasn't ready enough to be on the roads on four wheels, spinning around with confidence. I used to sit in the passenger seat, scared of every big truck coming by, as I used to think this was the end. Karl and Charley used to try to chill me out and would tell me I was going to be all right! But that would get me angry and I would explode. I used to shout at them and ask them how it would be all right. Why wouldn't we die in a car crash when we were stoned already and blinded? Why would you push me to get out of my house and die dirty, after having forbidden sex?

I had almost lost it. I started to advise Karl and Charley to retire, quit the dark life and stay with me. But at the same time, how could I advise someone not to do something when I was already doing it? How could I stop someone smoking cigarettes when the smell of my own mouth was smoky? How could I tell someone that having sex before marriage was forbidden when I had lingerie on my wall as decorations? How could I, when I had an empty box of cigarettes that had condoms and joints of hash inside it in my hand?

I told them I might not be the best example to give advice, but I was still the man of used, or second-hand, or refurbished principles and dignity.

The Orange Truck...

Time went by and I was still fighting for life and to get myself settled. Me and freedom were miles away from each other and I always doubted that our paths would cross one day, but at least I managed cut myself loose from my past of poverty.

I was living like a sinner, beast, infidel or faithless man. I gave advice about justice, religion, life, love, family, mercy, etc., but with a stoned voice and drugged, sad eyes.

Karl grew up and came to me one day, so excited. He said, "I am finally getting laid tonight!"

I said to him, "Please **DO NOT**."

"Do not worry about me. I can handle this," he said.

So I asked him a question. "You currently live with your family. Where and how are you going to do this?"

"I have no place to go. The only option I have got is to drive off to Alexandria, 200 miles away from Cairo, and rent a beach house and come back by tomorrow morning."

Karl was desperate and excited, and his silent eyes were begging me to not be mean to him and just agree with what he wanted. Whereas I knew something from when I was young, that I'd read once in a book that said, if someone left his home and was on the road heading to work, or to school to learn and study, he is blessed and kept secure by angels, or God, until he reaches the place he is heading to. But someone driving, at such speed, on a motorway in order to get laid; I think that would end up badly!

I told Karl I wasn't sure that he would survive the night and this was against the rules of life, philosophy, religion and everything.

He said, "Do not worry. I will drive smoothly and my car is brand new." By which he meant that the car was high performance, with new breaks and a stability function, which would help him to be safe and prevent him from having an accident.

I was surprised by the way he calculated and measured things! I told him, "Believe me, when you go against nature, nothing will stop fate from happening."

That night was first time Karl did not listen to me. He lied to me and he said that he was going to go out and would catch up with me later on. At 2:30 a.m. I was on my bed in my dark room, surrounded by smoke and sad music, spending my night relaxing. Charley walked in and he was a bit shy or nervous about speaking out loud and I asked him what the matter was. He said Karl had had an accident on the highway and he was now in the hospital.

I got dressed very quickly and drove 70 miles in less than 30 minutes, as I was racing to the scene. I saw Karl and he was trying to avoid looking into my eyes. He was covered in blood and was full of wounds, and said Je Je was in the operating room having 36 stitches in her forehead. Karl hugged me and said he was sorry and that he didn't think anything bad could happen. I found out from the receptionist at the hospital how the accident had happened. Karl had been driving recklessly, following a huge truck of oranges. The driver was heading to Alexandria to deliver the fruits to one of the warehouse farms and unluckily the driver lost control and flipped over with 50 tons of oranges at over 120 kilometres per hour, as this is the regular speed on the motorway, Karl was further behind doing a speed of 160 kilometres or 100 miles per hour. The oranges jumped all over the carriageway and into oncoming cars, running like tennis balls, squeezing juice all over the road, flipping cars and causing crashes. That day Karl believed that regardless of what the latest technology could do, it wouldn't have stopped fate from happening, just like technology couldn't stop the earth cracking or the flooding in Japan when it destroyed half of the country.

The orange truck became a wise and significant story in our minds, which showed us that your destiny could end up as a little piece of anything. Since that event everyone was convinced that I could feel and predict danger, and they all listened to me. But I was not a psychic, nor could I read the future, I was just applying the rules and theory of life. It's black and white. Life is about karma and I learnt that the hard way.

Karl loved the taste of money and the posh lifestyle, and he wanted to have his own. He slipped from the direct path and I heard that he started to travel around the cities, bringing hash and drugs from the coast into the city. I saw him a couple of times afterwards in the street, by accident, but he drove away to prevent my questions and also to avoid me letting him know that I was disappointed in him.

Every type of hash in the city used to have a name or a code, such as the flyover, the dance floor, skydiving and so on. Normally the name is engraved on the piece before cutting. Charley was the only one stopping by to see me, supporting me with expenses and crashing at my place for the night. He knew that the last thing I would do was sell my principles again and go and sell drugs like others. Everyone also knew that the last thing I would do was quit smoking hash, as this was the only medicine that helped me to maintain myself and resist my hard times.

But one day I heard that the new, fresh hash in the city was now called God. I exploded again and I quit smoking for the first time after five non-stop years. People were calling me crazy. I had to fight with all the people who smoked this stuff and tell them how we were being drugged slowly and had become slaves to those drug dealers. Now they had messed up and written the word God on drugs and people were still smoking it!

That was the end for me and I quit. I had old stuff, small pieces as a backup, but I kept them for emergency needs. But the funny part was when I got out of the house, while this new stuff was in the city. One day I was driving with Charley, heading out to get some food. On the way we stopped to see two brothers, who owned an antique shop and were good friends to Charley.

Charley was talking to one of them inside the shop and I was talking to his brother outside, and as a greeting they offered us two cigarettes of hash. So I was smoking and while I'm smoking and talking at the same time I was telling the guy about all this.

"Have you heard? About that stuff they called God!" He said yes he had. I said to him that it was messed up and unacceptable. When had human beings' values become so cheap? The guy kept silent and smiled. I went inside the shop and I told his brother, "Actually this is very good stuff. What is the name of it?"

He said, "It's called God!"

I told him, while I was still smoking, "No, no. I am talking about the one I am smoking now."

He said, "This is the one you are smoking now. It's called God."

I threw it away in his face and I started to shout everywhere, saying, "We have been sold out! We are done! There is no way back!"

They thought that I'd kind of lost my mind, as who nowadays smoked drugs with principles? That could sound funny and could make anyone laugh, but for me, I was crying deeply and appealing for human values that no one cared about any more.

I was the only person at that time who was living half broken and half alive. Particularly when I received a call from the past, as the past decided to be my enemy in life and death. It was a private number from abroad that was calling me.

I picked up the phone and someone said, "Hi, can I speak to Oscar?" I said to him that it was me speaking. He said, "Hi. It's me, your brother, calling you from London!"

I thought that one of my friends was having a nice joint and it had taken him so far away, so I said to him, "Who are you?"

He replied, "Damn Oscar, your voice sounds like a grown-up man's since the last time I remember speaking to you ten years ago."

I couldn't say anything to him, I was confused and my brain had gone blank. I had not talked to him, or seen him, for over ten years and I couldn't even remember what he looked like. I was speechless. I couldn't find the right words in the dictionary to describe my feeling at that time, I was so removed.

Especially when he said, "I would like you not to discuss the subject of what happened in the past. The only thing I can say to you is I'm sorry that I couldn't help you at that time, as I was young."

I said to him the same as I'd told my mother. "It's too late to apologize."

He said to me, "Please do not change your number and I will be in touch with you very shortly."

I was overloaded and I increased the amount of drugs I took, as I was destroyed inside and obviously on the outside too. My life suddenly became a storybook and something strange happened to me, my tears wouldn't come any more. I had seen enough and my river of tears had already become a drought.

He called me next day and he said, "I have an offer for you and this offer is a simple apology so you can forget what happened in the past. I will invite you to come to London and stay here with me for one month as a holiday. Then you can go back and finish your last year in university, then come back to London and I will pay for you to study and start a new life with a new beginning."

I said to him, "That's a great offer and a dream for anyone, but for me, I don't think that would erase what I have been through and it won't reassemble the pieces of my broken heart." I do believe that sometimes my heart needs more time to accept what my mind already knows.

A few weeks later Charley was gone. He had to go into the army to serve for one year and Karl was lost in the dilemma of his life. I was totally alone with Ammy, having the most painful sexual relationship ever and to escape from this illegal, forbidden relationship I had to accept my brother's offer.

I came to London in 2008 as a visitor for a month. I met him in the airport and he recognized me quickly, with a strange, excited smile, as the last time he'd seen me I was a kid. He was happy and I felt that I wasn't hiding in a bottle all my life any more and suddenly I'd come out and was surrounded by English words everywhere and colourful, happy tourists that came from all over the world.

He was mostly busy and I walked in the night around the London Eye with sad music in my ears, wondering, thinking, dreaming, moaning, but the conclusion I reached was that I needed to go back and finish my last year at university and then come back to London as quickly as I could.

But not because London is the best place in the world! In my case I had a different reason. The only thing that could help me to forget the old, painful times wasn't drugs, but to be in a different land, with my eyes and my mind seeing different people, smelling different scents, looking a different colours and experiencing different weather. A place where nobody knows who you are, your story, or where you came from.

The only solution for me was to be reborn, but on a different planet. If I could I would wish to change my skin, my name and click the reformat memory button in my mind. I wanted to delete everything that had happened in my life, undo the past and move on.

The month finished very quickly and I was dying to go back to gain my revenge. I went back to Cairo; Charley was falling to pieces, as his service in the army was not matching our lifestyle. But that was a great opportunity for me to go back to my college and put a plan in place to pass this year and fly to England!

I booked an appointment with the principal of the college and he was amazed, as he hadn't seen me for three years. He arranged a meeting with all my teachers and after a long conversation they assured me that it was impossible for me to recover and capture the three years of study I had already missed and just blend all of them together into one. They brought my three-year results together and what I had scored, by cheating of course. First year: pass. Second year: pass. Third year: pass.

I said to them in the meeting that I could capture the material for all of the three years' subjects, plus the fourth one, and score well, but I needed their help to give me the chance. They said that it would be impossible, but if it happened, I would be the hero of the university.

I was advised to meet one of the nerdy girls in the university, in order to sit with her, as she was one of the best students and she would be able to explain to me all that I had missed of the subjects and what I had to study in one year. It was a *Mission Impossible* task for me and all of them, but for me it was also a goal that had to be scored, as it was my only way to escape.

I invited her to my home and we slept together. We used to have sex, then sleep, then study for almost a year. After reading through all the dramas and novels, I was surprised and regretted that I had missed amazing subjects such as literature, drama, novel, poetry, prose, philosophy and phonetics. I admired Shakespeare plays and quickly I became a big fan of Dickens' *Oliver Twist* and the civilization that was England. I became an expert and I loved what I studied. I captured all the three years' worth of work in the fourth one and amazingly I scored a merit in the fourth year. At the graduation party day I was the university miracle and was awarded the best drama school student and a future young novelist.

Of course no one knew how I'd done it and what the reason was for this success, especially in all those literature subjects, but I am sure the person reading my book now knew why and how! That is was a miracle to pass and graduate in the final year of the BA.

But that wasn't the only miracle that I had to achieve, there was something else out of my hands. I was selected to be in the army for a year, as the army was compulsory. That was the time when I was truly defeated and I begged fate not to choose me, as I was already a soldier who was serving permanent duty in the war of life. I was in my final pain, battling in silence for freedom and praying to God.

Amazingly, life decided to give me relief and the month I was born wasn't selected to serve. I was out and ready to fly to London.

Alfred paid for my English course and also my flight ticket. I don't know if I was ready for this or not, but what I was sure about was that I certainly needed to escape to a different planet and start from scratch with fresh dreams and no pain. Also I was taught that sometimes what are you afraid of is the very thing that may set you free. Or perhaps I couldn't wait for the day when I broke up and said goodbye for good to the past.

Because all my life I'd been running away from someone or something, but had never got anywhere, the first thing I was planning to buy when I got settled was a big fish tank with goldfish, as I enjoyed looking at them. They made you feel calm with no attachments. Listening to their movement in the water reminded me of my blood running through my veins.

The day I made my way towards getting this huge plan was unforgettable for me. I was thinking deeply about how my experience made me painfully aware of the upcoming future. There is a huge difference between giving up and having enough, but I was done and was extraordinarily destroyed, both physically and mentally.

So Charley, Karl and Ammy drove me to the airport. Charley was so happy that I was leaving, as he wanted me to recover and have a pleasant future. Karl was in tears and getting sentimental and Ammy was falling down every ten minutes and begging me not to leave. Drugs heavily intoxicated me, I was holding on to my flood of tears and I was saying goodbye to the most beautiful land in the world.

Plus I was about to give my last speech, even when there was nothing left to say.

I deeply wanted to thank the past for all the lessons it had provided and I particularly wanted to tell the future that I thought I was ready.

Perhaps some of you will know these truths already, but for the people who do not, I would like to tell them that these are the lessons that I have learnt in my classes of life that helped me to carry on and survive.

I have also witnessed that sometimes when bad things happen in our lives, it puts us directly on the path to the best things that will ever happen to us, because in my life I have lived, I have loved, I have lost, I have missed, I have hurt, I have trusted, I have made mistakes, but most of all, I have learned.

I learnt that maturity comes when you stop making excuses and start making changes.

When you experience something bad, challenge it and do not ever lose; either win or learn.

Always pay attention to your gut feelings. No matter how good something looks, if it doesn't feel right, walk away...

I learnt the meaning of success the hard way. Success is about being able to go to bed at night with your mind and your soul at peace.

I learnt that often people who criticize your life are usually the same people that don't know the price you paid to get where you are today.

I learnt that givers have to set limits, because takers rarely do and if you are giving your all and it is not enough, you are giving it to the wrong person.

Some people create their own storms and they complain when it rains.

Keep going as each step may get harder, but don't stop because the view is beautiful from the top.

Telling the truth and making someone cry is better than telling a lie and making someone smile.

Be careful who you trust and tell your problems to.

Not everyone that smiles at you is your friend.

Strangers can become best friends, just as easily as best friends can become strangers.

Sometimes you have to move on without certain people. Not because you don't care, but because they do not.

Trusting someone takes years to build, seconds to break and forever to repair. Think twice before trusting someone who let you down.

If you love someone tell them, because hearts are often broken by words left unspoken.

People change for two main reasons: either their minds have been opened or their hearts have been broken.

Sometimes you have to let things go to give room for better things to come into your life.

Life is like a piano; the white keys represent happiness and the black show sadness. But as you go through life's journey, remember that the black keys also create music.

Remember: weak people seek revenge, strong people forgive, intelligent people ignore.

A broken promise hurts just as much as a lie. You do not just make them believe, you also make them hope.

Nothing hurts more than being disappointed by the person you thought would never hurt you.

I have never met a strong person with an easy past.

I usually give people more chances than they deserve, but once I am done, I am done.

You could meet somebody tomorrow who would have better intentions for you than someone you have known forever. Time means nothing, character means everything.

If you are not sure about your friends, hard times will always reveal true friendships.

Sorry is like a Band-Aid; just because we use it, it doesn't mean it is going to heal the wound.

Always, always trust your first gut instincts. If you feel something's wrong, it usually is.

Never waste your time trying to explain who you are to people who are committed to misunderstanding you.

Do not waste your time with explanations. People will hear what they want to hear.

You can't be strong all the time. Sometimes you just need to be alone and let your tears out.

Most importantly: Do not make a decision when you are angry and never give promises when you are happy.

Welcome To Europe

NB: this is my personal view as a writer and is based on my own experiences. I am expressing myself with no intention to discriminate, insult or diminish any culture, religion, gender or any other differences.

London

I remember the first time I landed in London at Heathrow Airport; I had no clue where I was going or what this part of the planet was like. Europe, the Middle East, Asia; all those regions for me did not exist, nor any other countries on the earth. I was sheltered from the entire world. I was living in my own abandoned planet. The only place that was familiar was the room that I used to hibernate in, feeling destroyed, broken and lost. I had learned a lot from the movies about New York City and as I was making my way to London, I was expecting this specific image in my mind.

On my way to London I was resting my head on the plane's window, looking at the sky with a strange feeling in my broken heart, there were no words to describe it, but I would say it was my first time feeling petrified of my sense of freedom. I felt like I was a prisoner who had just been released after a life sentence since birth and had just greeted real life. Or perhaps I felt like I had just woken up from a coma that had lasted many years.

It is not easy for me to reveal my story to anyone, so I chose to keep it to myself and I added to my list of forbidden secrets. But my eyes always betrayed me, hinting that I had something to hide. I remember my first day in London; I woke up early and went for a walk. It was a beautiful, sunny day. I ended up in Leicester Square, watching people sitting around the park, enjoying the sun, eating ice cream and feeding the birds. It was quiet and peaceful. Everything felt like a dream and I had no idea who these people were, or where they were from and on which part of the earth we were located. But they were so beautiful and colourful and friendly.

Believe it or not, I had no idea what British people looked like. What were their customs, or traditions, or even religion?

The only thing I knew for certain was that whoever those people were, they did not speak Arabic.

I had to set up a plan. How was I going to communicate and live with these English beings? The first thing I decided to do was to delete my entire history from my mind's eye, all the negative things my eyes had ever seen in my past, and to start afresh, using only the positive things I saw and learnt. And when I looked back on my life, I remember a shadow of an innocent child, fighting for his life; he'd had skills and talent, but no chances or opportunities.

Personally, I hate science fiction and fantasy, as I believe that it has nothing to do with reality and it blinds people from the truth. It misleads them, as it's full of one man's imagination and it is all based on technological skills.

The movies and the media portrayed London in a way that surprised my reality. I thought the city would be glamorous and sunny, full of white people, blonde girls with blue eyes, and luxurious 4 x 4 cars. But the reality was a big shock for me. I discovered that the media are skilled in dressing up reality and turning it into a fancy. And here was the reality of London.

Coming to London to study and work was a brave step to make, especially considering my language barrier. But I had nothing to lose, as everything I'd had had been destroyed, except for the innocent boy who had now grown up and was ready to take every opportunity that was thrown at him.

At first I was shocked when I saw so few English people in this city. Instead there were all these different nationalities, colours, cultures and religions. There were people from every corner of the world, all blended together in a big city. I was not too happy about this at first, as I wanted a full English cultural experience.

I asked my brother what the next step was. He said, "Apply for an English course. Then you must go to every shop in the city and give them your CV."

So on the first day I took the bus to Tottenham Court Road and I went to every coffee shop. I would enter Starbucks or Costa and I would try to hover in the background, till the queue ended, so no one could hear or see me asking for a job. But unfortunately, every time, the barista would walk by the queue and ask me how they could help and everyone looked at me, so I would just order a cup of coffee. I was so shy, embarrassed and proud. By the end of the day I was holding a lot of coffee cups.

My brother was angry with me, because I had been in London for almost a week, sitting at home and still I had no job. He was trying to convince me that being shy or sensitive was something negative that I must improve. Next day he took me to a hotel where the manager was a friend of his.

Well, when I saw his friend coming towards us, I read him immediately (as I was good at reading people at first sight). The guy started to attempt to intimidate me with his radio and he started to give orders to other staff members. He had a typical Middle Eastern mentality. I wanted to leave, but at the same time I had to stay till the end, to prove that this guy was misleading us. As expected, at the end of the day he said he would see what he could do and would let me know if there was a job available in the future.

My brother would go to work all day and I would sit home in the dark, listening to my sad music, as the past left me with a bitter, clogging aftertaste and an increased sense of being institutionalized.

Another one of my brother's friends worked as a chef in a local pub in Wimbledon and he offered me work to help him out in the kitchen, washing dishes, mopping the floor and taking care of the rubbish.

On my first day I put the kitchen uniform on and started to clean. I remember that night, after I finished work, I took the bus home. Tears fell fast and silently. I watched people, hoping that someone would speak up, telling me not to worry and hug me. I felt the same every night when I finished another shift.

I started to fight with my brother every day. This was not the job for me, this was not my dream and this was not what I'd signed up for! He didn't think I had a choice, that it was either cleaning dishes or back to the street. Every day I was in tears and felt as if I was bleeding from the inside; my high hopes were becoming exhausted.

One day a beautiful young British girl named Georgia came to work in the pub. I loved her from the first moment I saw her. The owner came to introduce her to us in the kitchen.

She said, "This is the chef, this is Arthur, this is Oscar – he doesn't speak English."

I was so embarrassed. I wanted to scream and say, "Wait a second. I can understand English perfectly and I can speak English at least a little bit."

It was like a bullet in my heart to be humiliated in front of this new, beautiful girl.

I used to help Georgia carry the wine bottles from the basement and offer her sandwiches. One day I went to the garden in my lunch break to have a quick cigarette and I saw her sitting alone. I was too shy to say hi, so I pretended I hadn't seen her. She called to me and said to come and sit next to her. I was so embarrassed by my kitchen uniform, as it stank of oil.

Instead I said, "Do you study?"

"Yeah, I study philosophy."

"That's really cool. Philosophy is the most amazing thing ever to happen in life to brighten up people's minds," I enthused.

"Yeah!" she replied, sarcastically.

"I used to admire all the philosophic opinions and how every one of them defined the freedom of his own vision and perception, but Descartes' perception was especially my favourite one."

She stood up. "No way! That's what I am studying now."

She could not believe that a non-English speaker, dishwasher and smelly boy could be that educated and talk about an important subject in philosophy.

I wished that I could have told her that I used to get full marks in philosophy and that I could write novels and essays. But my English was not good enough to tell her all that, my break was finished and my dirty dishes were waiting for me. I went home that day so excited and I started to tell my friend how I had fallen in love with Georgia.

He told me to ask her out for a coffee, but I wasn't brave enough to do that. A few days later I decided to write her a letter.

My friend laughed at me when I suggested it, and said, "She will laugh her head off, if you do that!"

"I know writing love letters is old-fashioned, but I always find it to be the most delicate and romantic way to express yourself when you can't speak. In letters you can say whatever you want with no fear of the other person reacting and you can express yourself entirely without facing any embarrassment."

So I wrote the letter and the day I went to work to give it to her, she was gone. They told me she had handed in her notice. I was not really looking for love, but Georgia was the only light amongst the dark and dishes.

I decided to leave the dishes and I gave my notice. I stayed home, shattered, disappointed, drained and hurting. My flatmate at this time, Emma, had been watching me for a few days, moping around.

"Why are you not at work?" she asked me one day, whilst I was standing in the kitchen, staring out of the window.

I exploded. "I am not a kitchen boy and that is not my

dream and this is not who I am." And my tears began stinging my eyes.

She walked away. The next day she knocked on my door.

"You are going to work with me in my security job." She had already spoken to her manager and he was expecting me tomorrow for an interview.

I went to the interview and I got the job. I put the uniform on and there was no kitchen hat and no oil smell. It felt right, at last.

I used to stay up all night in a workspace, office building or a hospital, watching CCTV footage and the dark sight of the night. I did this for two years, going to school in Covent Garden in the daytime and having the best time of my life. But when night came, I found myself waiting for the time I would be attacked or killed by armed robbers, or a gang would break into the building. But nothing happened. I was fearless and had nothing to lose, except some dead dreams that seem unrecoverable.

But once, on the late night shift, I had a call from my friend and this call wasn't expected. That night my patience had run out and my emotions were explosive and twisted in fury. I felt strong and weak at the same time. I was determined, yet broken. In the call I was complaining to him that I could not see any light at the end of the tunnel in my future job, or even in my normal life, and I felt so lost.

"Do you have any money to run a business?"

"NO!"

"Unfortunately, you're foreign," he told me. "Your max pay rate in England will be minimum wage." (Which was currently £5.82.) "And the truth is you are not going to get any more than that! You are a bloody foreigner in this country, so don't dream too much." And he said, "Even if you had a master's degree it wouldn't help you. So you are a security guard on £5.82 per hour and that is your destiny." He also said he could help me get slightly better pay (£6.20), as London Royal Mail were looking for a new postman.

"WHAT! This can't be it! This can't be!" I shouted down the phone. "You've lost your mind and you do not know who you are talking to. I am not a postman and I will never be. I am not going to deliver a parcel to a random house and their dog will run after me until he bites me in the ass. Just like my whole life has bitten me in the ass. It's not going to happen. I have dreams and I will be something and I will show you."

This conversation was around 4:00 a.m., but I felt something and I went back to my desk and created a CV for first time ever in my life. But the problem was what could I write? What experience did I have? I did not know what to write. I am good at cleaning dishes? I am good at crying?

That night I spent four hours sending my CV to every single vacancy on the Internet. I applied for some jobs which I didn't even understand the meaning of the job title. If there were hospitals that were looking for doctors, I was even sending my CV to them. I was desperate to find a job, or maybe I was refusing to let my dreams be buried again.

After that night, I phoned in sick for two weeks and hid at home. I was saying goodbye to all my dreams and telling them I was sorry, I'd really tried.

Ten days later, I woke up and I was on the train heading to Hampton Court Palace, food in my hand, with only plans to feed the ducks. While I was on the train my phone rang. I picked it up and an English girl was talking and asked me bring my CV and come for an interview tomorrow. I said to her to please send me the postcode and I would be there on time.

I hung up the phone and had no clue who I was talking to, or even what job I was being interviewed for. Next day, I got dressed for my interview in jeans and a shirt.

I took the Tube to the address she'd given me, rang the intercom and someone said, "Please come to the third floor!"

I went upstairs and the door was open, as I looked in I saw a spacious exhibition area, photos hanging on the walls of celebrities and models and rooms made only from glass. Handsome men in suits were talking into phones and beautiful ladies in short skirts and high heels were chatting and exchanging documents.

I thought I had entered the wrong place and I turned around to leave, when suddenly the receptionist ran after me and said, "How can I help you?"

"I had a call from someone to come for an interview." She said that it had been her and to grab a form and have a seat with the other candidates. I felt so underdressed, uncomfortable and not at all confident.

I passed through the smart ladies and gentlemen. I was sweating all over as I sat in between them. I said to myself, *I am going to embarrass myself* and I decided to leave immediately.

But before I could stand up an older, glamorous-looking woman walked in with a tiny dog and her assistant and said, "Welcome everybody and thanks for coming. Today is your first interview and if you pass we will contact you the very next day. If you do not pass today we won't be contacting you, so please do not call us or bother us at all and good luck in your life somewhere else."

How simple was that! I was listening but still had no idea what the job was or what I was supposed to do.

Her assistant then proceeded to instruct us. "Each one of you needs to stand up, read the questions on the board, answer them and sit down again."

I realized that when my turn came that was going to be the end of it and I would be kicked out, so I answered with no care or attention, but with a confidence, as I believed I was already going. I was short and confident because I was 100% sure I wouldn't pass the interview.

The first question was: If you worked at the most luxurious place in the world and they offered you a complementary item, what would it be and what would you pick? Secondly, what is the latest achievement that you have completed in the last few months?

Every girl stood up and said, "I would like a Louis Vuitton handbag."

Every boy stood up and said, "I would like a Rolex watch."

When my turned came I said, "I do not really need anything. I have got everything I wanted. And the achievement I have done in the last few months was getting myself in here, to this interview."

They said, "Thank you guys and we will contact the people tomorrow who passed this interview."

I walked away downstairs and as soon as I reached the street my phone was already ringing. I picked it up and I said hello.

"Hi Oscar, congratulations you have just passed the first interview. Please come tomorrow for the second interview, but with a professional suit if you could please."

I said to her, "You must be mistaken. Can I give you my surname to make sure you are talking to the right person?"

She said, "No it is you, the little Egyptian guy."

I told her that was correct and asked her how many people had passed the interview besides me.

She said, "In this afternoon's interview it is only you so far, but we have got one more interview session to run this evening."

I told her I would be there tomorrow on time and I called my brother, Alfred, to tell him the entire story. He said that it was definitely a scam, but that he would buy me a new suit and we would see.

The very next day I bought a professional suit and I was the smartest, good-looking guy in the entire interview.

After 20 minutes of chatting, the interviewer said to me, "It was an honour talking to you and it has been a very interesting interview. You will be sent tomorrow to (H), the most luxurious retailer in the world, in the fine watches department and good luck in your life."

I could not believe it that day and I ran into the street laughing loudly and smiling at passengers. I felt like I wanted to dance like Jim Carrey singing in the rain. Then suddenly I felt like crying and I remembered my favourite scene in the *Great Expectations* movie, when Ethan Hawke walked under Estella's house after his opening day, screaming out loud and saying, "I DID IT. I MADE IT. ARE YOU HAPPY NOW?" Though I was living the same scene silently in my heart and was talking to the past while everyone I knew flitted across my mind.

The Unstoppable Tourbillion

My heart and my mind decided to cooperate together and move forward without looking back, like a flying whirlwind or tourbillion.

On my first day I walked into (H) and into the fine watches and jewellery department. I had no clued about anything with regards to customer service or even the name of any luxury brands. I was like a newborn. When I walked into the fine watches room, I was not amazed with the bright crystals all over the place, the lighting or the jewellery; it all looked like an unaffordable dream. I was not impressed, nor did I feel that I wanted any of this; I just wanted to be found and discovered.

I remember Kat, the head of retail at that time, was the only person who was standing in the middle of the room. She looked at me with her incredible smile and asked me, "What is your name?"

I could not even remember my name at that moment, as I felt that I had just died and gone to heaven. When I heard her warm voice and saw her beautiful eyes I was lost for words, and when I looked at her body, I found myself in front of a unique masterpiece, a sculpture made by Michelangelo.

Kat was a very delicate and sophisticated young woman, but with a strong personality too. When she walked on her heels, her steps were like piano notes that must have been taught in Cambridge University, no doubt. When you looked at her you felt the world stop under your feet. You could also believe that she would never get old.

In no time I was all grown up within that room and in six months' time I knew it all. I was the best at customer service, exploring customer expectations and needs was my greatest skill, I taught beginners and introduced products and knowledge all over the place. I made sales in those six months of around 900K. I received more than three feedback comments from clients that changed my life. I was offered a full-time job with (H). So I had to leave the agency and worked for (H) directly, with a doubled salary. I loved the team and the managers, and everyone in the place trusted me a lot and supported me.

I was generating love wherever I went and was trying to be myself as much as I could. At this time I was the man on the ledge. I did not allow my mind to think even once and gave it a holiday. All that I used to do was wake up early in the morning, go to work and learn. My heart was the only thing that was allowed to think, react and judge. The following year, I made 1.2 million sales, scored 98% in mystery shopping and I was awarded the personality of the year of 2012 in the fine watches department.

I remember that day well. I was standing on the stage in the induction room, receiving that certificate and I was struggling to hold back my tears from exploding. I wanted to scream and cry badly and tell everyone about my story. I wanted to say to them I had finally won the last bid of my auction. I'd finally won my dignity back, I'd finally won my principles and I found my confidence again. That day I was just born again and I was the happiest man in the world. I felt that for the first time in my life I wanted to cry, but not from sadness this time. I wanted to cry hysterically from happiness. I felt I had revenge on the past that was chasing me. I felt that a few of my heart's scars had been healed. For first time in my life since I'd been born, I felt that finally I wasn't rejected.

I fell in love with (H), regardless of the quote, "Love is one of my favourite mistakes". But in my case, I had nothing to offer except love; the only credit I had in my heart bank, unlimited withdrawal, with an unlimited overdraft and no interest, and you could also take a loan for a long or short term. My heart was open 24/7 to people.

The second full year at (H) I made 1.3 million sales and I was rewarded again as the personality of the year for 2013. The feedback I earned from clients, managers, directors and colleagues completed the missing puzzle in my broken personality. With all the rewards and success I achieved in (H), it powered me up and recharged my dead battery. I also learnt a lot about fashion and I became extremely knowledgeable about every brand in the fashion world.

My client relationships were at their peak and I was promoted to brand senior ambassador in my third year and eventually I became the brand manager, with a high professional performance and a friendly vibe. All my fears were gone. Tomorrow did not scare me any more. In the end, the past was the only thing I would undo if I could.

The year after I was growing and shining every day and drawing my own dreams. I got married to the girl I wanted to be with and I would die in her arms too. I can't find enough words in the English dictionary to describe her, but her touch, when she puts her hand on my face, is just like a painkiller or medicine. Every time we go out together we always hold hands and feel like we are on a date. She heals my pain with her smile. She brings luck and blessings for every step I make.

I also bought my dream house and bought the car I used to fancy. I also bought two things that used to be little dreams when I was young. I always wanted a fish tank full of golden fish and a Spanish countryside guitar hanging on my wall. Finally, I got a novelist's desk with shelves full of books by Shakespeare and Charles Dickens.

I did it all; I was relieved and walked free.

The Luxury Dream And Life In Knightsbridge...

(H) is one of the most luxurious smaller "cities" in the city of London.

I called it a city instead of a store, as inside the place you are introduced to a world where a variety of different characters, from different nationalities and cultures, all live together under one roof, sharing their norms and values with one another:

Asian: (Indian and Pakistani)

They are the most hard-working people ever, with a non-stop work ethic and strongly value their traditions and customs. Some of them are such friendly and warm characters and some of them prefer to stick together and are very traditional.

I have found that Indians are very professional in retail business and they give all their attention to the business rather than the Pakistani members of staff.

Their personalities are quite often very humble, modest and down to earth, but they are very inquisitive and curious. If you said to one of them, "I have friend coming from Dubai. Do you need anything from there?" He would reply with a strange answer like, "Is he coming alone?" and "What was he doing in Dubai?" and "What colour of clothing is he wearing?" and "How much does he earn there?" and "Why is he coming to London?" and "Is he coming by bus or plane?" etc.... So they always like to know the details about everyone, even if they won't benefit from it.

Iranian:

They are smart, eloquent and very well-spoken individuals. They are very fashionable and stylish. They also have strong personalities, which I have sometimes found to be too demanding for me. The women are witty and feisty, and definitely keep you on your toes.

Turkish:

They are the most natural and humble kind of people. I love their country, food, culture, skin colour and humour.

Greek:

I would always describe them, with their addictive deep black ,eyes that they could take you miles away, and their dark black hair makes you lose your words in front of their beauty. Greek women are very family orientated and they make perfect wives, with their combination of an amazing beautiful appearance and elegance, along with their power of feminism. Pretty and sweet as sugar, sensitive and they have a jealousy streak that represents their protective stance. They are strong on the outside and soft inside. I am in love with their eyes, characters, country, culture, weather and salad of course.

They are those types of people who once you met you feel that you have known them forever.

European: (including English, Greek, French, Russian, Latvian, Lithuanian, Spanish, Italian)

I have found most Europeans to be extremely hard-working and dedicated to their jobs. They are very tidy, clean and well presented. They are also very family-oriented.

On the other hand, I have found that some Europeans, who had never had a taste of the luxury life back home in the small, old-fashioned villages where they originated from, come to (H) and fall in love with the type of lifestyle they see around them. The crocodile designer bags, the beautiful Italian handmade shoes, the sparkling diamond watches and necklaces, the lavish marble flooring and grandiose chandeliers. A small minority of these people become so obsessed with this lifestyle that they are willing to sell their principles and dignity to have a small taste of "the good life". However, their thirst for wealth and extravagance is never quenched and they are never satisfied with what they manage to obtain.

Other Europeans, like Romanians and Bulgarians, especially the women in my experience, have less glamorous jobs, such as call girls or sex workers. The majority are attractive and are people that you could get married to, as despite all of this, some of them are decent and beautiful woman.

Middle Eastern: (including Algerian, Moroccan, Egyptian and Tunisian)

From my observations, the Middle Eastern members of staff are extremely hard-working and generally very polite, friendly and charming. Some of the guys love to admire the beautiful women who shop or work at (H). They are also very curious beings and love to know everything about everyone, even though sometimes it may not concern them.

The Little City

In the (H) induction they said to us that (H) was a little, small city. I thought they were just exaggerating their description, but after few months in (H) it was clearly a small world just like the one outside. (H) was just like a miniscule version of London city for me.

You see also a lot of different mentalities of humans being "staff members" and "management". For some of them their suits make them blind and they start to act very arrogant and always walk around with their hand in their pocket, looking at their shoes all the time. When you look at them they pretend they are looking at their phone, to avoid embarrassment and I think that's because back in their country they would never have got to a position that would allow them to wear a suit, unless you were a doctor, or prime minister. Or perhaps it is a normal reaction to the excitement of working in such a luxurious place as (H). Or perhaps those who walk around in a suit with their hands in their pockets think that the suit covers their internal, mental excitement, but their body language would always tell the truth. I call them the switchers, as they try to be like bears, changing the colour of their skin depending on the weather conditions, but in the end they are still bears.

So in my opinion, England helped all those people to grow and reach their dreams, but they still could not change their mentalities.

British Born

These are the people who were either born here, or originally came from a sophisticated family and you find them very modest and humble, and always willing to help. When you see them in suit, you feel that they wear it the same way as they would if they were in casual clothes, without any changes in their personalities.

The Dreamers

The young women and young men who come all way from poor cities in Europe and come to London to work hard, seeking luxurious Louis Vuitton handbags and Chanel watches, while at the same time their family back home is waiting for a small ripple of money so they can afford their living costs, as they struggle to feed themselves.

Some people like that get very weak and susceptible, they always get caught up with fashion and they become addicted to it, as it makes them feel better and they convince themselves of that. For some of them their dreams are much bigger than that, such as the gold-digger types, as they hunt for a rich, stupid Middle Eastern guy who might take them for a ride in his yellow Lamborghini, as girls nowadays do not believe that the man with the white horse is enough compared to the Lamborghini. In the opposite way, you will see a Middle Eastern, older man taking advantage of this by coming to (H) hunting for a starving lamb, who needs to be fed in a five-star restaurant and have a Chanel bag as a gift, then she pays him the price at the end in his hotel bedroom.

In Knightsbridge you meet people who have lost their dignity, principles, culture and even religion, and have become slaves to the luxury, supercar lifestyle. You come to (H) to see the most beautiful and expensive jewellery, served by the best selection of the hottest girls from all over the world as well. Is (H) the dream of every single human being on the earth? It also could be a nightmare for other people at the same time. It can reflect your view of your own humble life and you could start to hate it. Or there are other types of people, who work hard and spend all their savings buying expensive clothes, watches, shoes, ties, suits and perfumes, just to match their surroundings and environment, and at the end of everything they have nothing left except their fancy, valuable accessories, hanging in a wardrobe, in a rented single room in Stratford and when time goes by and they go on holiday back home in five years time, they bring shame to their family, as they did nothing with their life.

In Knightsbridge you also meet all types of people from across the world, famous celebrities, footballers, rich, poor, politicians, Mafia, traffickers, prostitutes, dreamers, insane, thieves…

And you will also meet special customers like G.S. and M.K. The two characters that changed my view of life and the way I think.

Greg S. is one of the most famous and successful business traders in the world. When I met Greg, I did not know who he was at the beginning, but I saw myself, over the next ten years, in that man, full of energy and modesty, very friendly and joking with everyone non-stop. He is one of those kinds of people who really enjoys himself and loves life. He made my day the first time I saw him and I named him the customer of the year.

Afterwards, when I knew that he was a millionaire, I was shocked, as the way he reacted to life was absolutely amazing and humble. I admired his personality even more. Greg unintentionally showed me another form of being rich that day, his heart and his character were so classy and wealthy.

Musi. K was the simple little man who walked into my boutique and unexpectedly added something incredible to my life. He currently plays a large role in my life, similar to the character Robert De Niro plays in *Great Expectations,* as my secret benefactor.

It is very difficult to describe that man, but the day he walked into (H), and my department in particular, was beyond any expectation. I saw him browsing around, wearing simple clothes, and clearly you could see the shyness in his eyes. A semi-smiley face and his modest voice were so unique. I greeted him with hospitality and at the end of our conversation he purchased his 19K watch from me.

I was a bit surprised that he could afford this watch, as the modesty and courtesy in his character would never let you think he could be that wealthy. After that we kept in touch, and he made more purchases for his family and friends, and I discovered, after getting to know him well, that he could afford to build and open his own luxury (H) if he wanted to. So he was that rarest of things a "diamond in the rough" if you will, a wealthy young man with the greatest of hearts, which brings us to the same conclusion and a new definition of being rich. It's not necessarily the price of the coat you have that makes you rich, but it's the size of your heart that does. We became very good friends in no time and after knowing him for almost three years, I discovered that money for him does not make any difference to his personality. But helping people was what made him the happiest..

Musi has that trait of buying something he does not need or won't wear, but he buys them just to give as gifts and to help others in a way that won't break their dignity. Some people have proud personalities, when you offer to do something for them, or help, they feel offended or uncomfortable with themselves. Musi has the skill of helping people in such a simple way. He will also go out of his way to help; he would drive his supercars miles and miles away just to aid someone.

He has a good spirit and warm heart, even with animals. He has got several dogs that he looks after and they are quite important to him. The way you see those dogs approach him, you can understand immediately how generous this man is. I was so overwhelmed by having contact with people such Greg S. and Musi K. who changed my view of life and renewed the definition of wealth and richness, at least for me.

Overview Of London The City

One of the questions that crossed my mind immediately when I lived in London was how amazingly the British government set up such a system to force and commit all those varieties of human beings in one direction, to respect and follow one set of rules, considering the language difficulties.

I was really amazed how smart those people were – as I naturally admire smart people – especially when you see those English police officers on London streets and the way they are trained to deal with all kinds of earthly human manners, in a polite and self-controlled way, which for me is more than a police job. It makes those officers, for me, more like psychology doctors.

One thing about London is that you can find yourself visiting the whole world without travelling, if you want to. If you have never been to Asia, you can simply visit Chinatown and you will have a full Chinese experience for certain. Even if you want to visit India, you can go to Stratford. For the Middle East, you may have to go to Edgware Road and Knightsbridge.

In London you can experience the European culture, as you will meet a lot of Russians, Lithuanians, Polish, Latvians, French, Italians and the little cities of Europe. Some of the European women that I have come across who work in luxury retail, look absolutely stunning and well presented, but in my experience I always found it hard to connect with them on a psychological level. I just found them to be absorbed in matters that never concerned me, such as materialism.

Regardless of this, you may initially think that you will never change your feelings towards them, but in fact you will fall in love with them. Here is my first poem to one of the European girls:

I Promised

I promised I would tell the truth and I found myself being guilty for too many lies.

I promised I wouldn't.

I promised that I wouldn't lie to you and I did.

I promised I wouldn't betray our friendship and wouldn't fall for you and I did.

I promised I wouldn't think about you all night long and I did.

I promised I wouldn't miss you when you were gone but I did.

I promised I wouldn't reveal my feelings and I did.

I promised I wouldn't allow my heart to love you and I did.

I promised I wouldn't write a poem about you and I did.

I promised I wouldn't tell anyone how beautiful you are and I did.

I promised I would keep all my promises to you and I did not.

I promised I wouldn't send you my words but I did.

London for me wasn't as I had expected, but in a way it was an amazing experience to be added to my buried library, it increased my ability to deal with more and different kinds of people, along with the kind I was raised with, and now it's much easier for me to communicate with more confidence.

I would say that London as a city, eventually needs only smart people, in order to survive and develop, but as people are always scared of change they tend to stick with their current job and end up as a 50-year-old and still working as a security guard in a workspace in the city.

To be honest there is so much to learn and so much information reaching anyone's mind to learn about the world's cultures, geography, manners and traditions. London is also the city that can make you fall deeply in love with people you have never met before. In fact some people get so attached to their best friends and loving relations back home that you would never think that you could make such a strong relationship with anyone else other than your old mates, but in London you will be surprised that you can make friends and they will be the best friendships you ever had, even though they're from different parts of the world, with different nationalities, religions, cultures and different languages, of course.

So that brought me to a conclusion, that I now don't consider English a language, but in fact it's a link connecting people with each other in one city.

In London you also say goodbye a lot to people who you've met for only a short time, but your heart has already attached itself to them, as London is a temporary place for some people and when they leave they take your heart with them. Some of them come here to study, or work, or for money, then they head back to their home. Personally, I consider this to be one of the hardest negatives to deal with here in London, but with social media you still keep in touch more often. In London you will learn how to be open-minded towards other sexual orientations, such as gays, lesbians and others.

In fact, based on my upbringing, I was slightly prejudiced towards same sex relationships, since it was uncommon back home in Egypt. But when I met Edward, the Irish millionaire, he said to me one day my perception would change. In fact Edward was right, and my perception has now changed entirely, especially after meeting Matt and Alex.

I find myself feeling guilty for initially having judged people, especially when these very people have helped me to learn and excel in my life and career. They were Matt and Alex D., who is in fact the person editing this book right now, and who knows all my secrets from birth.

One thing to love about London is that you will learn a new form of communication, which is love. So it's very common to find two different nationalities married and having kids, yet their English is not good enough, but they still carry on with life and understand each other perfectly using eye contact.

London will open your mind to the world of politics as well. You can easily find a Palestinian working with a Jew, or an Iraqi with an American, or a French person with British.

London is the craziest place in the world. It is so extreme in everything, love, sex, friends, work, politics and even crime. With regards to English people, I have lived in London for almost six years and I have noticed that English people are less racist than any others and the reason for that is their education. British people are well educated and they have read and learnt a lot, and have travelled extensively, so when you introduce yourself to them, surprisingly, you will find they know where you come from and what your culture is about. I have found them to be very polite and respectful of other people's races and cultures. I have also found that the British accent is the most charming and brilliant form of spoken English. I have to admit also that English people are extremely fair and always give second and third chances to other nationalities to grow up and achieve. They are also very calm and have enough patience to endure any unexpected reactions from others, that's why they always find a solution for any problem, as they've got the secret to solving anything, which is calmness. In England dreams can be achieved and come true, either if you're a singer, or talented somehow. Smartly and quickly they will discover what you're talented at and they will put you in the place you deserve. Or to make it simple, they appreciate any talent or skills in the first place.

In England you can easily be discovered and become famous and rich in a short period of time. I would love to call England the land of the mysterious dreams.

English people are also the source of modesty and humbleness. In England it's very common to see a judge, who is in charge of a court, cycling in the morning in cheap trainers and running to get to his job, and you would never know who that cyclist was; he might be a millionaire and have millions of pounds in the bank, or he could be a politician or an actor. You see those types of top people queuing up for the Tube and waiting for their turn in the supermarket, or any other public place. Every day you could see someone of high rank, or an owner, or even a director of a big company, which would give them the right to be arrogant or show off, but you see them cleaning the floor and helping the rubbish man, or painting their house by themselves.

Whilst in other cultures, these high-ranking individuals would be chauffeured around in their limousines, puffing their cigars, whilst wearing sunglasses all the time. For some of them, money has made them blind and made them forget that they are human beings, just like everyone else. I remembered how back home in Egypt life was entirely different; some of the rich who had high-ranking positions and were extremely wealthy could be very arrogant. Ultimately they abused their sense of humanity and they offended people of lower classes, thinking they could buy humans, but they failed to buy love, sense, friendships and manners.

As a conclusion, I was losing the will to live there and nothing was perfect, and as a result, I admire the English mentality, as everyone is equal.

When you go further outside London, you may feel slightly alienated due to the reactions you may receive from people. I wouldn't say it's racism, but rather, people may find the way you look, your skin tone, your hairstyle or your dress sense is different to them, since many rural areas around Britain are inhabited by mainly English people. For that reason they may stare at you, which might make you feel slightly unwelcome. But in reality, they may just be analysing you, since they don't often come across people with such features.

Personally, I had not experienced, or even felt, any kind of unwelcoming talk, or any hint of racism, but in fact I had to do my own research, just to discover either if I was mistaken about British people and I'd just got a good eye, or they were racist. I had to find out. After I had seen some videos on YouTube and I had been to some places, such as Maidenhead near Heathrow Airport, as I had been advised by a close friend that there were some nice views there, such as horses and green Thames scenes, I was really surprised that people were looking at us oddly and in fact I was driving my decent, semi-expensive car and my wife and I were well dressed. Once I reached the Thames we spotted a nice multi-level coffee shop on the waterfront of the river. As my wife and I started to approach the cafe, we couldn't help but notice the way everyone was staring at us. We immediately turned around, got back into the car and left.

I assume that the main reason for British people to be sometimes prejudiced towards other races is that they think immigrants are taking their jobs and places, and are benefiting from the government's kind system. According to my own fair judgment I totally agree with them, as it's quite difficult to live in your own country and have strangers walking around with better jobs and houses. But in reality I disagree with this view, as a small minority of British people do not go into further education, but still expect the highest salary. This is against business ethics, as in the United Kingdom your job rank is usually determined by your qualifications.

I have found that many businesses and investors opt to hire foreigners, as they accept minimum wage and sometimes they may also work harder. In my opinion, they probably work harder because they appreciate the opportunity they have been given here in the United Kingdom, as back home they may not have been able to get this job or even earn half of the wage that they are being offered here. However, I'm neutral with regards to who wins this argument, as I understand and empathise with both sides.

I also understand British people's attitudes towards foreigners that take advantage of and abuse the benefit system.

Some foreigners are also accused of evading tax from which they make a ridiculous and envious fortune. You usually see them driving around in the latest and flashiest cars, and buying the most luxurious watches.

But the person who we should blame is the government and the system's kindness. You cannot be so kind and give housing benefits, child benefits and job-seeking benefits to people, who in their country can't even have half of that, and they still have to respect their country's rules, otherwise they have no other choice or option. So being kind and amazing with the wrong people, in the end, you will indeed get humiliated and disrespected. If you were a father and had a teenage daughter and you spoiled her, she simply could swear at you in front of anyone. Even in relationships, if you become so kind to your girlfriend and give her anything she wanted, I would tell you, congratulation, you are going to be dumped very soon. It is the nature of human beings.

British conversing has always intrigued me. After coming to London and speaking with many British people, I observed that the most common phrases you will hear are: "How was your lunch?", "What did you eat?", "Oh, that looks nice.", "What's your plan for tonight?" and "What are you having for dinner?"! I would never have considered talking about food because in my opinion we eat to live, not that we live to eat. However, in time I have come to admire the simple nature of British conversation and small talk, which usually revolves around the weather, last night's dinner and what's on television. I have discovered that this is part of British etiquette and is a token of courtesy.

Another topic that fascinated me about the British culture was what was considered as fun. I always considered the simpler things in life to be fun, such as, enjoying the company of my best friends, making jokes with them and having deep and meaningful debates with them. I also enjoyed taking strolls along the river Thames, feeding the ducks and playing with my dog. However, my greatest joy was making other people laugh. If I could bring the slightest bit of happiness into someone's day, I would feel satisfied. However, I soon discovered that here in London it was quite a common thing for people to work very hard from Monday to Friday and leave all of the fun for the weekend. Their idea of fun may be partying, drinking, skiing or whatever else. I found that "fun" had a different definition for almost everyone, depending on his or her interests and hobbies. I would hear all sorts of crazy and exciting stories from my friends, such as, going on a weekend binge drink, having a one-night stand, ending up in a hospital after having their drink spiked, or waking up the next day in a complete stranger's house with no recollection of the events from the night before. To my surprise, my friends would easily pass off the antics from their wild weekends as, "just a bit of fun", without showing any feelings of regret or guilt. One thing I learnt from them was that life does indeed move on and there's no point dwelling on one's mistakes. Instead, you should always focus on the lesson that emerges from any situation and apply this to your life.

Similarly, I discovered that in the city of a million cultures, not everyone shared the same traditional ideas about love. What is love? What makes you love someone? Is it beauty? Well, I have sometimes noticed that people fall in love with someone's physical beauty, as opposed to their inner beauty, such as one's personality and characteristics. However, I have also observed that for some, a common definition of beauty has become more sexualised and beauty can be measured by the size of one's intimate parts, or even how good they are at performing sexual activities. Even wealth is sometimes considered to be a measure of attractiveness.

Thus, some may be attracted to others for more sexual reasons, or even materialistic reasons, as opposed to romantic connections. Perhaps the act of holding hands has become old-fashioned and blow-jobs have become more preferred.

Even music itself has eventually followed some of these alternative definitions of love. Before, when you listened to a song, the rhyme would capture your heart and remind you of good memories, or a time with an old flame. But nowadays some songs have to be seen, not heard, as their music videos exhibit what some consider as physical beauty, such as muscular men and fit women, which can distract you from the sentimental and emotional meaning of the song.

I used to think that sunny days were made for a nice walks with a cold drink in a park, or for feeding the birds, or playing with the kids or dogs. For some of us it's a great day for cycling, or travelling on a long driving trip.

It is also quite a common sight to see people wearing bikinis or swimming trunks in a public park, whilst sunbathing or reading a book. Whereas my idea of reading a book was sitting at an old English oak desk with an ancient-looking desk lamp, surrounded by old books standing on dusty shelves, written by novelists and famous authors. I came to learn that Britain is a land of freedom, where most people have wonderful, open-minded attitudes. So although back home in Egypt where people are more conservative, wearing a bikini in a public place would be frowned upon, in England this was completely acceptable and normal.

Even the smallest of things, such as exchanging gifts with friends, brought me a surprise. With Christmas gifts for example, the people who surround me have told me that I could buy underwear as a Christmas gift. In my view, a gift has to be something very sentimental in value, or remarkable, or romantic, or express something, but underwear is not in my dictionary and not on my list of options. In my opinion, I feel as though gifting underwear conveys a sexual meaning.

I cannot deny that I am a huge fan of Ann Summers and Victoria's Secret. I'm not trying to be judgmental here, but I'm appealing for the real taste of life, which we used to know and to review the way love should be described. Or at least we shouldn't be overwhelmed by the new generations and feel guilty for our mistakes. I'm trying to protect the decency of human taste, before humanity becomes just like animals or just a memory, as unfortunately I feel sometimes sexuality has become the main judging factor of many things in our lives.

Even in business environments, management used to discuss figures and targets as a measure of the candidate's skill and achievement. Based on my own experience in retail, I have noticed that some retail agencies' requirements focus nowadays, not on skills or customer service experience, nor what is on your CV, but rather they focus more on appearance and body figures of their employees. It is quite sad indeed, but I have personally witnessed this when I went through an agency to get into retail. They made the female candidates walk and turn around, in order to measure how pretty and sexy they were, as this could benefit the business by attracting customers for better purchases.

One of the things that I personally find hard to understand in England is the people and the government's attitudes, which are very sensitive towards sexual harassment, or any hint of sexuality. I have found that in London, on the rare occasion, you could quite easily have intercourse with a girl that you just met in a pub or a club. If you paid for the drinks in return, this could happen on a street corner, public park, on public transport, in the evening or in broad daylight, in private, or even in front of people. To some people, it really doesn't matter any more. The only thing that does matter is not to lose the opportunity to have sex. Which leaves me to wonder; has real love-making become so rare that it's a moment of the past?

Sometimes you will also see on public transport, especially when it's late on the weekends, loads of people wearing more inappropriate clothing than usual. Perhaps, since people are on their way to dinner functions, clubs or bars, they wear attire, which may be quite revealing. You may find you get slightly excited and you may decide to take a peek, as it is our natural instinct. However, if you make an inappropriate remark or approach the person, you could end up in trouble with the law. This, for me, does not make any sense at all. For me, the English expression springs to mind; these people who are exposing their bodies have *shot themselves in the foot*. I certainly believe in self-expression and dressing in whichever way you please, however dressing quite revealingly in certain places, such as on a train, is likely to cause you unwanted attention.

I have also noticed some parents have been complaining about inappropriate behaviour from teachers towards their children in schools. The fact is that sometimes the parents themselves allow their teenage schoolgirls to wear inappropriate clothing, like short skirts or low-cut tops, and then they complain that their daughters always get harassed. Or maybe the girls wear these types of clothing without their parents consent, and in that case schools should monitor pupils more closely. Despite the fact that the schools here in England are supposed to be religious. For me it was something hard to understand, it is like someone getting naked in public, taking a shower and then complaining that people are looking at them and breaking their privacy, which does not make any sense.

In fact I read an article in the *Daily Mail* newspaper and here are the highlights: "School bans girls from wearing skirts because it's distracting for male teachers when they walk up stairs or sit down." July 2015.

Some people might say my views sound like those of a religious man, but in fact I am not religious at all and I never have been. My answer would be simply, read my autobiography and you judge for yourself. But we need to believe and face the fact that temptations do exist, as we are human beings at the end of the day. Let's think about it like this, you may walk around an art gallery and admire all of the beautiful paintings hanging on the walls, but you are not going to buy them. In the same way, looking at an attractive person who is exposing their assets is not completely taboo.

It is the beauty of that person which creates the temptation in the first place. So my next question is who is in the wrong here, the painting or the voyeur?

British People

Personally, I have found them to be the most attractive, beautiful, hard-working, professional, sophisticated, educated, smart, romantic, sensitive, protective, humble, friendly, supportive and totally independent people who can be relied on. They are most grateful for the simplest of gestures, such as a simple compliment, a small gift or a flower. When I first moved to London, interracial relationships were foreign to me because back in Egypt we didn't have much racial and cultural diversity. So when I noticed that sometimes British men would marry women from other cultures, such Chinese, Japanese, Thai, Polish, French, Italian, Spanish or Russian, the reason was totally understandable. Some women from these countries are more traditional or old-fashioned and prioritise homemaking and family life. Whereas some British women, who are just as amazing, are more career driven and more modern. Some men may feel insecure and challenged by a powerful and successful woman. Or perhaps, they prefer the food!

Another observation of mine is that some English people can come across as introverted to some people. They enjoy their own company and like their privacy to be respected. I understand that some celebrities or public figures may shun the public, as they do not want their lives plastered all over the news, but why would a regular person require so much space and privacy? How would one expect to make friends, relationships, get married or integrate into society? Back in Egypt it is common to find that most people, even those who have never met, can easily engage in a conversation whilst sitting on the bus. However, in London, I found that people on the train avoid eye contact, look right past one another, bury themselves into a book, or stare blankly into space whilst listening to music. This is probably one aspect of British life that I don't enjoy because I'm a real people person and as I'm living here I'm concerned that one day I too may lose my open nature.

What drives me even crazier is that the British only like TEXTING. So if you decide to call, or to phone someone to discuss something, you are really making a huge mistake. So the rules seem to be, texting only and reading a book. But later I understood, after personally living here, that at work you do a lot of verbal communication and as we all go through tough days at work, you get that feelings of switch off and you just need to relax and not talk. Maybe that's why texting is the only way. In comparison, I have observed that some British people are completely the opposite when it comes to their pets; they are very attached and devoted to their pets. They are fed generously, walked multiple times a day, and petted and stroked generously. Sometimes I wished I were a dog, to get the attention that they give to dogs here in England.

But some of the British are extremely amazing and get attached to other nationalities, trying their food and customs, and you really will fall in love with them immediately. They have a sense of humour and a friendly vibe too.

Some people think because the British are quiet and polite that means they are stupid. I would say absolutely not. They are very smart and intelligent indeed and that's why they are quiet and polite. I have tried to learn from them and work on my own personality, adding this valuable aspect into my character.

Also in England protecting a person's human rights has effectively allowed some thugs, criminals and gangs to control London's streets at night. In fact they could be a bunch of kids under 18 years old, and sadly they could easily end someone's life by stabbing them with a knife and destroying a big family, including a wife and kids.

But I believe that nothing is perfect, otherwise London would be a part of heaven, if some negativity didn't exist. The only thing that normally shocks me is, at the end of it all, the prison sentence that these criminals receive is far to lenient , spending their time playing video games and watching TV, and once they are released they go back on to the streets and the chances of them falling back into old habit's and the old way of life can be quite appealing to some if they haven't rehabilitated during their time in prison , because the punishment was so soft, short and entertaining its as if they haven't learnt their lesson and wouldn't be so bothered if they committed a criminal offence again..

With all the negativity you could find in England, I have to admit that I have fallen in love with Great Britain and the strange thing is that every day you fall in love with this city. Some people come to England illegally and pay some Eastern European a huge amount of money just to get hold of a British passport, as the British passport has all the benefits which can make their lives safer. But for me, England was not about a piece of paper (a passport), but what I earned and learnt that could be written on paper. But I would have the honour of having a British passport, just to say that I am proud to confirm that my heart is half Egyptian and is honoured to be half British, as England has become a part of my heart and Egypt always has been in my veins.

I have heard many things from people who don't appreciate their living standards here and try to ruin my image of British life. They have said to me that historically in the past, England has stolen many countries' gold, money and other valuables. Thus, Britain used the riches to develop themselves and created Great Britain. Then later on they allowed all those people, from all those countries, to come and work and serve them.

As an Egyptian I felt offended hearing this, so I phoned up my brother, Alfred, immediately and I asked him if it was true or not. He said to me that many things have been said in the past, some of it was true and some was not, but not to feel down as Gamal Abdel Nasser, the old president of Egypt, refused to allow the Egyptians to go and serve others. I felt more relaxed about this as my book is based on dignity matters and I thought I was the only person who cared, but I felt proud that I belonged to Egyptian blood. In the end I reached a conclusion. Let's assume if England had not stolen anything in the past from those countries and life had just carried on, I would think that their government would already have stolen this money, as every country has got corruption or a bad president. But for England, investing this money or gold and growing this money, and then bringing people to work, live and benefit from it, it is a kind of apology as well. So from my point of view that was the best thing England ever did. Sounds like a loan England borrowed and paid back in a better way.

Someone else said those people suck our blood like the taxman! I used to say to them, look around you! The tax you are paying lets you be comfortable to use public transport and allows you have a good clean view of parks and trees with no dirt, like in your own county, so be grateful! Some others always say "this country" or "those people" and I used to get very upset when I heard those words and would say to them, "If you don't like the country why are you here?"

And when someone says "those people", I aggressively reply, "Those people accepted you in their country with a smile, whether you are Muslim that may wear a scarf, or Jewish that may wear a shtreimel, despite whether you are a non-English speaker or not. Just let us remember that those people and this country helped you and me to have a better lifestyle here than anyone could dream of, with less effort you could have a nice car, or the latest iPhone, which in some countries you could spend most of your life working just to afford them." I just found myself hating people who did not appreciate what others did for them.

Before we judge or criticize, we should think and take a good look around us, be fair and do not forget that England also makes people hate their own countries somehow, but with no intention of doing it. Some people come to the UK and live here, but after a while and a bit of adjustment, once you get used to the living here, they normally don't realize how their living has improved till they go back home for a short holiday, then they start to compare things such as manners, systems, cleanliness, food, transport, affordability etc.

For example, in England if you have any complaint or problem to discuss, they always try to help you and make your life easy and simple, whereas back home your problem may get ignored and you may have to start to use different ways to solve it, like a bribe. Then some of them start to count the moments until they go back to the UK, where they feel safe and happy, and they get upset once their holiday is finished.

In the end, personally I find Britain is an addictive place with no doubt and British people are adorable in their manners. I have found the British to be sophisticated and educated, friendly and funny, and you would adore them no doubt, and you will have a space and respect in their life. After six years of living in England, my personality has already changed and I'm overwhelmed by their courtesy. My personality has become a mixture of two elements, or a combination, of a strong Egyptian sense of humour and history, and British manners and sophistication.

I always wanted to be rich, go back after years and award everyone who stood by my side and tell them thank you.

I always wanted to tell all the British people, thank you for having me in your country.

I always wanted to cry and say to the past, thank you for the lessons.

I always wanted to smile and embrace the sky between my arms.

I always wanted to tell humankind, be happy, we are so lucky.

I always wanted to talk to my heart and tell it, thanks for never leaving me alone.

I always wanted to tell every girl I knew, I am sorry and

thanks for being a part of my story.

I always wanted to tell my wife, thanks for choosing my station to be terminated at permanently.

I always wanted to tell my friends, thanks for enduring my anger and accepting my presence.

I always wanted to blame people for admiring photos and pictures of forgotten flames.

I always wanted to tell every pretty girl, thanks for sharing.

I always wanted to tell every educated person, thanks for existing.

I always wanted to tell my dad, sorry for not being put together normally.

I always wanted to tell myself, well done for resisting and not falling apart.

I always wanted to give my tears a permanent holiday.

I always wanted to thank flowers for decorating our life, not asking for something in return and being silent.

I always wanted to tell the future, I am really scared.

I always wanted to tell life, have some mercy on us and thanks for making us emotionally lost and attached.

After receiving feedback on this book I will be starting my new chapter in a brand new book, talking about life after marriage and how love in time could be driven into fine love, or routine, after few years of marriage, and why people cheat!

Sometimes we have heard that the common reason for cheating can be when your partner doesn't provide what the other partner needs, but in my new book I will be talking and explaining, in a great level of detail, about a rare reason for cheating that I have discovered lately. It is a small percentage but it exists with no doubt, it's called, "sick of perfection". It is a very interesting topic that touches our life every day and leaves us torn between silence and painful guilt. It also leaves us with too many questions that have no answers.

Here are some of the chapters that are going to be in the new book:

- The beautiful sins
- The orange door
- The cheating thoughts
- The forbidden daydreams
- The acceptance

Summary:

The Beautiful Sins

In my pervious book I spoke about love, hate, loss, sins, fate, loyalty, dignity and mainly morals, but after finishing my book I realized and experienced something else happening in our lives, such as painful feelings and unfaithfulness. We always think that marriage is the only solution for commitment and the only way to settle, or perhaps we thought it was the way to escape from life's temptations. Or to be clearer, we thought that marriage was the permanent protection from any upcoming or unexpected sins.

Today I am going to write about real feelings that I have personally witnessed and as a result, I was torn in this life between silence and painful guilt. I also blamed all the famous novelists and big philosophers for dying without leaving us with complete answers for humanity's questions.

We believe in a soulmate and real love, and we all go ahead with it once we find the one. But with time and age, we slightly feel guilty once your heart cheats on you and your thoughts start to swerve to someone else!

We feel guilt toward our partners, we feel sorry for ourselves and we either start to resist and step back, or some of us just follow the transmission and normally end up badly lost.

The Orange Door:

I did write a principles and dignity book before and I thought I had defined life with it, all the elements from outside and inside, and I thought my pen had terminated there. A few months later I didn't expect that my pen would show up again with another story, once my thoughts had dragged me to the orange door.

Once upon time and all of a sudden, you hear the sound of high heel steps that become the end of your resistance and loyal destiny! This is the moment when you see your heart falling on its knees, your strength melting, your mind stops immediately and you get lost gradually. This is the moment when you will witness yourself as a victim in front of her incredible voice and your tongue will lose the words when you look in her eyes. Your body shakes once you smell her scent and you nose dreams of touching her hair, while your eyes close. And suddenly you start acting like a little kid and you look and sound so random.

She looks at you at this moment, with no clue to what's going on with your senses! She will think that you might be creepy, weird or a freak and then she will start to respond to your strange actions; she starts to embarrass you and you get hurt...

Suddenly your strength wakes up, you gather yourself once again and start to defend yourself! You can't blame her for not understanding you! She doesn't even understand how her beauty destroyed you and all your senses, while she just stood next to you! She did not know that her smile made your heart smile too.

She walks away with no mercy! You decide to show her reality and how powerful you are. You also walk away without an explanation of what her beauty did to you! In the meantime you feel petty about her, as she missed what you felt towards her; it was real and it was only on your side.

After a couple of days you wake up from the greatest dream ever and you realize that she has got a partner just as you do. You accept the reality and go back to life with a broken mind, still thinking about her. The following day you feel like a poor sinner, guilty for something you haven't even done. You have not cheated, but you hate your heart for falling apart for an eye that never belonged to you!

And the next day you feel like a cheater, guilty. You are suffering in silence for a crime you haven't done physically but your heart did it emotionally.

Please feel free to email your feedback, comments or any questions you have in mind and you would like to ask:

principles.and.dignity@gmail.com

19254795R00067

Printed in Great Britain
by Amazon